SPIDERS OF SPY

MAX THORNTON

Published in Australia by Silverbird Publishing Pty Ltd.

First published in Australia 2025
This edition published 2025
Copyright © Max Thornton 2025
Cover design, typesetting: WorkingType (www.workingtype.com.au)

ISBN: 978-1-922958-92-1

The author has chosen Max Thornton as his pen name for his journey through life and when writing exciting fiction novels. It bears no resemblance to any other person who may have the same name.

With the exception of those who have given permission to use their names, the names of people and places have been purposely changed or deleted.

This book is for my children: Trevor, Kerri,
Shelley and Stuart.

You are too big to hold in my arms now,
but I will hold you in my heart forever.

Be grateful for your life. Every day is a gift you were
never promised, so make the most of it before it's too late.

Contents

Prologue

(Continuing from *Hardly a Challenge, Book One ...*)

Max and Jane had retired to Fairview. Joey had also retired but remained close friends with Max and Jane. Brian was still in the military as a Warrant Officer with the ASIS (Australian Secret Intelligence Service). Nitro (Bob) was in his last year as a driver with the Government Security Protection Service and Joey's father, Mick, had retired from GMH (General Motors Holden) and had become the 'Mr Fix It' man for the group, along with Joey who was a genius when it came to cars and their performance. Although Mick was well past the age of doing the work himself, he was now more the advice man on how to do it. Apart from Max and Jane, the group lived in various suburbs around the metropolitan area in downtown Melbourne. The families all came together for a weekend every three months at Max and Jane's place at Fairview. Although Brian and his wife, Emma, known as Em, had known Max for fifty years, they were still the newest in the group, as the others were Max's childhood friends.

Max's voice had deteriorated due to a cancerous polyp

that was removed from his vocal cords. After radiotherapy treatment, his voice now sounded like corrugated iron being dragged over gravel. When Max answered a telephone, he needn't say who he was; his voice did it for him. Anyone who knew Max knew at once who it was.

Chapter 1

I t was the middle of December 2007, and the weather had been extremely hot. Not unusual for years gone by, but it hadn't been this hot in recent years till late January or February. It was a Friday and Max and Jane were expecting the group for the weekend, the last one for the year, a bit of a melancholy Christmas get-together for everyone.

Jane had planned a barbecue on the lawn overlooking the Ninety Mile Beach. Max had been instructed not to let Nitro and Brewster burn the oyster blade steak and over-grill the prawns like they usually did, or burn the barbecue plate till you needed a shovel to scrape and clean it.

The first one to arrive was Joey and his wife, Lois. He had bought one of those two-seater three-wheel motorcycles. It looked like it had started life as a normal motorbike but with an extra wheel added and had been stretched like a rubber band and stayed that way. The people that 'designed' the camel had obviously had a lot to do with this trike, a perfect vehicle for someone like Joey sitting in the front seat as there would be little wind resistance, but Lois looked like she had been on the Big Dipper at Luna Park for four hours. It had an intercom system in each helmet so the two riders could talk to each other, but sometimes Joey would forget to plug his in and Lois would be talking away for hours with no response.

As Max and Jane got closer to look at the trike, a voice from the trike said, 'You are inside my security space. Please move away.'

'Christ,' Max said, 'what's next?'

Nitro and his wife, Marie, arrived at the same time as Brewster and his wife, Susan. They had decided to come together in Brewster's Chrysler 300C – black, of course. Brian and his wife were last to arrive, which was unusual; it was usually Joey and Lois who were always late. Joey often had to set the house clocks an hour fast to get Lois anywhere on time.

It was getting late in the afternoon, so they started to set up the barbecue for later. Jane said, 'Hey, Max, there's two cars coming in. One is Brian's BMW and the other one following is an MP Military Vehicle.'

'Must be one of Brian's MP friends,' said Max.

'Why would he be bringing whoever it is here?'

'Who knows but I bet we're about to find out.'

As they got closer, Max said, 'Jesus, it's a red cap MP Colonel. What's he doing here, for Christ's sake?'

'Hello. Sorry I'm late,' said Brian. 'Let me introduce Colonel Nathan Merrywether who is my Commanding Officer. He has heard so much about you lot he has decided to meet you over a steak and a beer. And, of course, he would like to discuss a matter of national importance with you. While Em is bringing some Christmas presents from the car, I think we should have a drink and get stuck into the barbecue. The Colonel will explain exactly why he is here, once we settle down.'

It didn't take long for Joey to notice Max was wearing a wig.

'Hey, look at this, you lot. Well, I'll be buggered! Max is wearing a bloody wig.'

'Trust you to be the one to announce that,' said Max. 'Well, I haven't got much hair left and it makes me look ten years younger than you, Joey.'

'You wish!' said Joey.

'Enough of this bullshit,' said Brian. 'I think it's time we hear why the Colonel is here.'

The Colonel said, 'Anyone here heard of the FLC?'

They all shook their heads.

'FLC stands for "frontal lobe chip", a computer microchip that interferes with the part of the brain that controls decision making, memory and self-control. Designed last year somewhere in Asia, most likely in China, only two were made. Both of them plus the brain switching device called the control module and the surgical wiring procedures have disappeared somewhere on the dark web.

'Once this microchip is implanted into a person's brain, their actions can be controlled from a distance by someone with the control module. Imagine if this chip were inserted inside a fighter pilot's head or the commander of one of our destroyers, they could be instructed to fire missiles and unleash all sorts of havoc. Our intelligence tells us that Russia and Middle Eastern countries have their secret service agents working on a plan to go after the chip. We certainly don't want them with their hands on the frontal lode chip package!

'Our intelligence has unveiled information that points to military personnel, both serving and retired, involved in the movement of these FLC chips into Australia for custody and pick-up in exchange of a large amount of money. There are three islands off the east coast of Australia where we think this exchange will take place. The Military Police have been tasked with the surveillance of an island off the coast of Eden in New South Wales, over 450 kilometres from Sydney. Last Chance Island, where we think the drop-off will be, is twenty-seven nautical miles, or fifty kilometres, off the mainland. It has an area of approximately 300 square kilometres and has a population of approximately 1,500 permanent residents, another hundred or so with holiday homes on the island. There is a small three-room schoolhouse with two teachers and a bush nursing hospital with one doctor and two nursing staff. The small township has a hotel–sports club, and a mum-and-dad type general store, petrol station and general car repairs and servicing all in one. There is a car ferry service once a week that delivers the necessary stores, fresh supplies and fuel, repeat medical proscriptions for the people at the retirement village, and other essentials that have been ordered. The retirement village has thirty retirees and operates a small bus and also owns and maintains the emergency pleasure cruiser. There are certain positions on the island that we have managed to keep within our resources for a civilian surveillance covert team. Brian tells me you people would be the perfect fit.'

'Jesus,' Max said, 'do you know how old we all are, Nathan? I'm the oldest at eighty and the youngest are in their bloody seventies. I don't know about the others but I'm way past the Mission Impossible stuff!'

'Well, I won't lie to you, although you would basically be just passing information back to us, there's always the possibility that things could go wrong. So, to keep that possibility to a minimum, we want to use ordinary retired people like yourselves, and we would have two retired trained military personnel in the group, being Max and Jane. I would at least like you to discuss it among yourselves and sleep on it. I'll come back in the morning for your decision. I am hoping for a *favourable* decision, as having met you all, you would be a perfect fit into the island's community without causing any suspicions.'

*   *   *

The girls thought it would be fantastic.

'What an adventure!' they said. 'We don't have to do much – just keep our eyes and ears open and pass the information on.'

They discussed the pros and cons of the covert operation. Nitro's wife, Marie, wasn't all that keen but she would go with the flow, and Brewster knew it wouldn't be as easy as it was painted to be, but they would all give it a go. Lois would take her teddy bear, and Sue would find a doll for Joey.

The next morning, the Colonel was pleased to hear they had taken up the challenge.

'Thank you for your support.'

They all said in unison, 'Hardly a challenge!'

The Colonel explained the pre-departure plans.

'You will all need a code name or nick name when talking to our network on the secure line. Give those names to Brian and he will pass them on. Having now met you all, this is what I propose. Max will be the emergency tour cruiser skipper and Joey will be his first mate and handle boat maintenance. Bruce will be the plumber and maintenance man at the retirement village where Nitro will be the village bus driver and gardener. Jane, you will be a nurse at the bush hospital, Lois will be teaching at the kindergarten and Sue at the school for grades one and two. Brian, you'll be in charge of radio communications on the mainland and Marie will be the radio operator communicating with twice daily check-in.

'You will be given the necessary credentials for those positions before you leave. Max and Jane will be given a military Browning 9mm pistol and a Sig Sauer 7.62 rifle for the group's protection if needed. For the rest of you who wish to have a weapon, we will assist you to get 9 mm pistols from a private source, and you will then be taken to a military indoor range to familiarise yourself with the weapons. You will conceal these and only use them for your personal protection if deemed necessary.'

They then chose their code names. Max became Wiggy because of his wig. Brian was Wing Nut as he had big ears. Bruce was Brewster, Bob was Nitro, Marie was Sparkie for doing radio comms, and Sue would be known as Auntie (she had always been called Auntie Sue). Joey was Slim, Lois was Slowpoke, and Jane as Tuppence.

Max said, 'We need to start using these names now to get used to them.'

The next morning, a military Humvee vehicle with blacked-out windows picked them up to take them to the military weapon testing indoor range at an undisclosed location. When they got out of the vehicle, they were already inside the building, so they had no idea where they were. Weapons similar to the ones they would be taking to the island were laid out at each of the shooting lanes along with an instructor at each lane. The Colonel and Wing Nut were up in the observation booth where they could view the results.

Each shooting lane had a Figure 11 twenty-five metre target at the other end. They were on a slide and could be brought back to the shooter to examine the target after the shoot.

The range practice began with Auntie trying to cock the pistol, holding it in the air and shooting one of the ceiling lights out. Slowpoke was in the next lane and managed to shoot three holes in her handbag.

Up in the observation booth, the Colonel thought, *Christ, I hope these people never have to use a weapon. At least the others have come up with average scores, so that's a plus. I hope we're doing the right thing, sending these people on this mission.*

Chapter 2

The two men, known to each other, sat separately in the passenger lounge at Singapore Airport waiting to board Singapore Airlines Flight 312 to Sydney. They each had one microchip in a sealed box labelled 'Hearing Aids'. At the same moment, the man entrusted with the control module, made to look like a small transistor radio. waited in the lounge at the Manila Airport for his flight direct to Melbourne. They were members of a worldwide ring of an underground system called The Syndicate. Its members were from all walks of life – lawyers, government officials, high profile members of the public, and the lowest of the low, thieves and murderers. The three men were well aware that if anything went wrong with their mission, they would be dead before nightfall.

Pham Linh was in possession of the surgical implant wiring procedures written in a language she couldn't read. She had already flown to Australia from Vung Tau in Vietnam. Her features were what Wiggy called harmonious. She had soft facial structures in a thin face with double eyelids and long, straight, black hair. She was now settled in as a tourist at Eden on the east coast and awaited the weekly ferry to the island. Her application for the job as cleaner and general duties at the retirement village had been successful. She too, was well aware of the retribution from The Syndicate should she fail in her part of the mission.

*   *   *

Back at Fairview, the eight geriatrics were calling themselves the Straight Eight Spiders of Spy.

'What a bloody joke,' Max said. 'There's not a straight one among us. Look at us – we're all old, bent and twisted, and in more ways than one. All this cloak-and-dagger stuff is way out of our expertise, whether they want to admit it to us or not. I'm telling you, we will be mixing with some very bad people, and these people will be playing for keeps. Let's not get all gung-ho – that goes for you two, Brewster and Slim: no bloody heroics! We have been close friends from damned near childhood, so let's see if we can all go our lives' distance together. Just do what we are asked to do, and we will all come home safe.'

They all said their goodbyes and went home to pack. They advised anyone who asked that they were going away for a short break with friends. They had been allocated a two-bedroom flat among a group of flats on Ocean Road on the island and they would arrive at one-week intervals, presumably not knowing each other. Brewster and Auntie would arrive on the island first, followed by Nitro and Sparkie, then Slim and Lois, and last of all, Wiggy and Tuppence. The only people who knew who they really were was Wing Nut and the Colonel. Once the group had settled in, the Colonel would arrive at Eden and run things with Wing Nut from the holiday house they had rented in Eden.

* * *

The Russians had sent three men and two women from their own version of the secret police, the ruthless KGB. Their location was unknown, but they would certainly be on the island or somewhere close by.

The two men sent by The Syndicate were met at Tullamarine Airport by a car and driver, holding up a board with the prearranged sign that said, 'Hawk Eye'. No words were spoken until they were in the car. Bruno was a well-built but scruffy looking fellow with a large scar that ran from the corner of his eye down to his chin, but even the tailor-made suit he was wearing did nothing to hide his bad and arrogant manners.

He said to the driver, 'I'm waiting for your update.'

'Yes, sir, everything has been arranged. There is a small Piper PA-28 Cherokee aircraft waiting for you at Essendon Airport. We will be there in fifteen minutes, and it's forty-five minutes flying time to Bairnsdale in Gippsland. The truck with the items you requested is parked at the terminal with the keys hidden on top of the front offside wheel.'

Bruno's offsider, known as the Ferret, was a scrawny, mean-looking man, one of The Syndicate's many hit men. He was a man who rarely spoke but would kill in a flash and think nothing of it. Both these men had been given their weapons by the driver and now had a familiar bulge in their jackets.

* * *

The Spiders of Spy had all moved in and met their neighbours, and publicly met each other for the neighbours' benefit.

Nitro was familiarising himself with the area surrounding the retirement village and Brewster was checking the emergency generator and hot water system located at the back of the main building when an Asian woman came in and began checking pipes and electric wiring. She hadn't seen Brewster as he was between the main generator and freshwater storage tanks.

He said, 'Can I help you? This area is off limits. Who are you and what are you doing here?'

'My name is Pham Linh, and I have just started work here as the cleaner. I was looking for the brooms and the mops.'

'Well, they wouldn't be down here, and you're not to come here again.'

Jesus, he said to himself, *I saw her checking the pipes and wiring. Very bloody suspicious. I'll let Nitro know and he can watch her as well, and Sparkie can pass her name on to Wing Nut.*

Wiggy and Slim were down at the jetty eyeing off the emergency and tour launch which they were now both responsible for regarding its operation, maintenance and cleanliness.

'Look at this boat,' Max said to Slim, 'Must be government sponsored. The village couldn't afford this.'

It was a forty-eight-feet Riviera Open Flybridge with twin Caterpillar 600 horsepower shaft-driven diesel engines, with a top speed of thirty knots. It had three separate cabins and accommodation for six people. Her name was *Mystery*, and she was certainly in a class of her own. She could eat up the twenty-seven nautical miles back to the mainland without a fuss.

'Shit,' Slim said, 'can we drive this thing?'

'Well, we are going to have to, mate. That's what we are supposed to be here for, so we will take it out all day if we have to until we are experts and we know everything about her.'

The first thing they were going to do was to stow the rifle on board. They couldn't carry it around and the boat seemed like the appropriate place for it.

*　*　*

The man from Manila had arrived in Melbourne and was on his way to Eden on a Greyhound bus. He had the control module and was the second link in the dark web's transport chain. He had obtained employment at the treatment plant for sewage, The Ferret was the third and final link. When all the pieces were together on the island, they would wait for further instruction and the arrival of the mystery buyers. Iran and Cambodia would have a finger in it somewhere, and our own secret service knew that Russia were after the chips, but there was still no intel on the KGB whereabouts.

Bruno and the Ferret had picked up the truck full of tools and equipment and were on their way. Their cover was to prepare the small aircraft island runway ready for bitumen, although once everyone was in place, they didn't plan on being there long.

*　*　*

Slim said, 'Jesus, Wiggy, this boat can really move!'

They were moving through Herring Bone Strait which took them from the calmer waters off Eden to the rougher waters of the southern side of the island, where the ocean swells beat against the rocks at the bottom of the high cliffs. It would be impossible to launch or retrieve a boat along this side of the island. As they cruised past the cliffs, Slim was scanning the outcrop with the binoculars.

'Whoa, whoa, hold it, Wiggy. I need a better look. I thought I saw something.'

Wiggy swung the boat back.

'Shit, mate, take a look and tell me what you see.'

Wiggy took the binoculars.

'Holey moley, looks like there's two bodies down on the rocks.'

On the way back to the jetty, Slim rang Sparkie and passed on the message to be given to Wing Nut. The police air wing and rescue helicopters arrived that same afternoon and winched the bodies up from the rocks. There was a crowd of locals on the cliff top watching all the action. The police made their usual worn-thin comment: 'Move along now, nothing to see here.' Those sorts of comments were treated as a bloody joke, particularly when the crowd standing there could see two dead bodies. The bodies were flown back to the mainland at Eden for identification.

The next morning, the radio squawked, 'Spiders, do you copy? Over.'

'This is the Spiders. Send message. Over.'

'Spiders, this is Wing Nut. Be advised, parcels delivered yesterday were for Mavis and Bert Fairweather, the previous general store managers who, it was understood, had left for mainland Eden last week with the retirement village manager. Be careful and stay on listening watch. Wing Nut out.'

In the eyes of the island locals, the Spiders of Spy had

become friends since arriving on the island, so it wasn't unusual for them to be seen together as was the case tonight at the hotel for dinner. Slim came back from the bar with the drinks and spoke.

'I've been speaking with the barman, and he said it seemed quite strange that Mavis and Bert just suddenly left. They were here and then just gone the next day, and then out of the blue, the new managers just materialised. But we know they didn't just leave, did they? And what about the retirement village manager? I wonder what really happened to him. These new store managers do not mix much. They keep to themselves. The barman thinks they're from Europe somewhere.'

'Very interesting,' Brewster said. 'I might introduce myself at the store tomorrow and see what sort of a feel I get.'

* * *

The truck with Bruno and the Ferret arrived on the weekly supply ferry. They had two rooms booked at the hotel and would start their work on the runway tomorrow, but today they had someone to meet. The Ferret paid a visit to the retirement village and left a note in the broom cupboard for the cleaner. The note said, 'Pool toilets need cleaning, take four buckets.' After the Ferret left, Nitro saw the manager read the note in the cupboard and put it back where it was.

At 4 pm, the Ferret and Bruno arrived at the pool to find Pham Linh, the cleaning woman, floating face down in the pool.

Bruno said, 'There are other players on the island, and they now have the surgical implant instructions! We still don't have the three pieces all in one place, but neither do they. Whoever they are, they will pay with their lives.'

Pham Linh's body had to be taken across to Eden, and because she had been employed by the retirement village, the launch was used. Slim and Wiggy watched as the body bag was taken on board. When they arrived at the marina, the police and coroner were waiting. Sparkie had notified Wing Nut of Pham Linh's demise and the estimated time of arrival of Slim and Wiggy. They were to meet Wing Nut at a place out of town for coffee.

* * *

The Syndicate man from Manila had arrived in the Greyhound bus only to find from the workers at the Marina that the supply ferry wouldn't be leaving for another four days.

'Is there any other way to get to the island?' he asked.

'See that cruiser there? It will be goingback there sometime today, but you'll have to wait till the crew come back.'

* * *

Slowpoke and Auntie considered themselves relatively safe at the kindergarten and school. The information they were getting from the kids was priceless but of no value to their mission. The fact that young Mathew had caught his parents with no clothes on wouldn't be seen as valuable information. The chances that either of the girls wouldn't have to use their gun was fortunately good as Slowpoke would have shot some kid's schoolbag and Auntie could have accidentally shot the teacher in the nuts. Tuppence was also in no immediate danger at the hospital, even though she was probably the best shot of the group.

'I'm not too worried about that,' said Wiggy. 'We will soon get her out of there if we need the fire power.'

The boys had coffee with Wing Nut. The only intel they had on Pham Linh was she had arrived in Australia last week on a three-month work visa to take up the position on the island.

When they returned to the boat, they were approached by a man who introduced himself as Felix. He said he was a manual labourer and had a job on the sewer farm on the island, and he was hoping he could go over with them. They shook hands and he came on board.

On the way back, Slim said, 'This Felix bloke is no manual labourer. His handshake was like a dead fish. Look at his hands, how soft and smooth they are. They're not the hands of a manual worker.'

The next few days were uneventful. Brewster went to the general store to look around. A large woman with short, cropped hair and an unusual amount of facial hair was stacking the shelves. She introduced herself as the manager's wife and said her name was Annika. She had large hands and a vice-like grip when they shook hands, and she was definitely from somewhere in Europe. The husband was outside serving petrol, so Brewster waited and introduced himself. He said his name was Nikolai, and as they shook hands, the hairs on Brewster's neck stood on end. He knew immediately who they were and what country they came from, and in his mind, this place was starting to look bloody dangerous.

The Spiders decided it was time to share what intel they

had so they organised a barbecue on the lawn at the unit's gas barbecue. They would be out in the open and the conversations wouldn't be overheard. Nitro told them what he had seen and was convinced that the village manager was somehow involved in all of this. It was even possible that he had killed Pham Linh. Although Nitro had met the man, he had only introduced himself as Brian. They would ask Wing Nut for further information about Brian. Brewster passed on his find at the general store and they all agreed that something bad had occurred there that had led to the murder of Mavis and Bert, the previous managers. You didn't need to be too bright to realise the current store manager and his wife were Russian and were up to their neck in what was going on. All of these findings were passed on over the secure radio link and the request for who the retirement village manager was. Although the girls seemed to be out of harm's way, it was suggested they kept their weapons at work in a locked drawer close by.

Brewster's transport round the island was a three-wheeled Agi bike while Nitro had a modified electric golf cart with a small tray on the back for his equipment. Slim and Wiggy shared the Toyota twin cab ute. The school was next to the hospital and only a short walk from the flat they were staying in, so the girls always went together to and from their workplaces.

*   *   *

Bruno and the Ferret were left to themselves at the island runway, which was far enough away from the populated areas as not to be of too much notice regarding what they were doing. They had unloaded and put together a small, motorised machine that was designed to detect lumps on the surface of the runway and grind them flat. It also had two other attachments to jackhammer and dig a narrow trench across the runway halfway down its length.

Brewster was on his way past the runway and small airport terminal shed to see where the drains from the village went and how they got to the desalination plant. As he skipped past the runway, he saw the truck and the workers. He decided to say hello and let them know who he was. As he got closer, he realised he had not met these men, and they weren't staying at the flats. They saw him coming and turned the machine off. He introduced himself and took an immediate dislike to them both, and although they were wearing overalls, it was obvious the one that called himself Ferret was carrying a weapon.

'What's happening here, fellas?' Brewster said.

The one with the scarred face who called himself Bruno said, 'We are here to level out the runway before they come to do the bitumen. This machine we are using grinds off the high surfaces and checks the levels.'

'So why is it digging a trench across the runway?' Brewster asked.

'We're putting in a cross-draining system before they do the bitumen,' Bruno said.

'Well, I'm the island's plumber,' Brewster said. 'If you need anything, let me know.'

As he drove off, he said to himself, *Why you would want a bloody drain across the runway like that? I'm buggered if I know. Anyway, not my problem.*

Chapter 3

Somewhere in the republic of Iran, Osmar was going over the last-minute details of his mission. He had in his possession three separate bank cheques. Each bank cheque was for the items to be purchased: the two chips, control module and the surgical instructions. He was to be the courier of $250 million for the exchange of the chips, control module and surgical instructions, but there were special instructions for the exchange. Osmar needed to get in and out of Australia undetected and to this end, the plan had taken more than a year to put together.

He would fly from Shiraz to Darwin on a British passport under the name David Rawlings, as a uranium mining engineer on a visit to Rio Tinto. Once he cleared customs in Darwin, his travel within Australia would all be by private aircraft: Darwin to Quilpie in outback Queensland on the Bulloo River, Quilpie to Broken Hill, Broken Hill to Bendigo and then on to Bairnsdale. The return trip would be the same. As far as his passport was concerned, it would appear that he had never left Darwin. His destination in Australia was six and a half hours ahead of his time, which wasn't a big issue.

On arrival at Bairnsdale, a car and driver would be waiting

for the last leg to Eden in New South Wales. Unbeknownst to Osmar, the KGB had infiltrated the Iran travel plans and the driver was a KGB operative.

*   *   *

The morning radio check revealed the retirement village manager's name was Boris Sokolov but he was known to call himself Brian.

Sparkie said to Wing Nut, 'That means there are three Russians here now that we know of, so it's obvious that this is the island where the transfer will take place. Due to the intel you people have been passing on, we have moved a back-up team and equipment with air support here just out of Eden and will be standing by if and when anything happens.'

*   *   *

The three Syndicate men were now on the island, but the fourth member, Pham Linh, was dead and the items she carried were missing. They decided to casually bump into each other for a 'say hello' meeting when they went to the hotel for the evening meal. Having introduced themselves to each other for the benefit of the other patrons, they bought their drinks and sat together at a table in the far corner of the hotel. They told Felix that Pham Linh was dead and the documents were missing. Bruno took control of the conversation.

'Before anything else happens, we need to put these items in one safe place. It's become obvious there are other interested parties after these items. There are three suspects of a European background, and we were warned about the Russian interest by The Syndicate when we left. I'm only guessing, but I bet the storekeeper and his wife are Russian KGB and they won't be here on their own. We need to resolve these issues and reclaim the documents before the buyer arrives, or the transfer will not go ahead and we will all be at the bottom of the ocean.'

That night at the flat, Tuppence said to Wiggy, 'The nurse I am working with has been very strange lately. Although she appears to be quite nice and she knows her job, there is just something not right. She speaks perfect English, but I've heard her off by herself speaking a foreign language on her phone.'

'What is her name?'

'Gail, but I don't know her surname.'

'Okay, let's get her checked out with Wing Nut, just to be safe.'

The Spiders were all together at Nitro and Sparkie's flat when the radio squawked with the message that the nurse's real name was Galina Soloyova.

'Jesus!' they all said. 'Another Russian.'

'Right,' said Slim. 'Let's do a count of who we think is on this bloody island. The storemanager and his wife, the manager of the village, and now the nurse – that's two women and two men we believe to be Russian.'

'What about the two blokes working on the runway?' Nitro said.

'They're not Russian,' said Brewster, 'but they're up to no good.'

'And what about the bloke we brought over here, Felix?' said Slim.

'I don't think he is Russian either,' said Wiggy. 'He is also up to no good and I wouldn't be surprised if he is in bed with the two on the runway.'

Slowpoke said, 'So who was Pham Linh, then?'

'Well, she certainly wasn't Russian. I'm betting she was part of the other three. Let's pass all this on to Wing Nut and they can play with the puzzle.'

* * *

All the Russian operatives on the island had been issued with the Russian Makarov pistol. Annika also had a one-shot lipstick pistol, fired by simply pressing it against a person's body. It was so small and insignificant it had no problems going through customs.

All the items for exchange with the buyer were now in one place with the exception of the surgical implant documentation. All the small packages had been placed in a container and inserted into the end of the pit that now ran across the runway. The pit had a steel cover that could be slid open by a small electric motor built into the end of the pit and operated remotely.

The nurse who Tuppence worked with had her suspicions of what was going on at the runway and she knew the transfer of the chips would likely be by air as a small aircraft could come and go from here at its leisure. She had been going to the runway at night to see what was happening. Unfortunately, she had been seen on one occasion leaving the area by the Ferret, and he followed her the next night. Galina was feeling her way along the steel plate across the runway with a torch when a voice said, 'Well. hello there.'

She looked up and the Ferret shot her between the eyes with his Glock pistol. The round came out the back of her head, leaving a large hole bigger than the one that went in. He loaded her body into the truck, and the body of Galina Soloyova was last seen going over the cliff and into the Pacific Ocean.

*   *   *

Osmar flew into Bairnsdale with Rex Air. He only had one bag, a Gladstone handcuffed to his wrist on a short chain. The man waiting for him nodded, and Osmar followed him to a black Mercedes AMG GT top-of-the-range luxury model. Osmar opted for the back seat for the four-hour trip to Eden so he could close his eyes and rest.

Just before they got to Cann River, the driver asked Osmar if he could stop to stretch his legs and have a smoke. Osmar agreed, and they swung into a picnic area. The driver got out and lit up a smoke, and Osmar got out and walked a few paces away from the car.

'Goodbye, you camel driving shit,' the driver said and shot Osmar in the back of the head.

The driver quickly found the keys to the handcuffs and the number sequencing to open the bag, The body went into the boot to be disposed of when he got to the coast. In the Gladstone bag were the three cheques, four passports and a copy of a receipt for the hire of a jet ski and an aircraft and pilot for a day, the flying time details to be advised. He would now adopt the identity of Osmar for the exchange of money for the merchandise on the island. He carefully inserted his own photo into one of the passports and headed for Eden.

*   *   *

Auntie, Slowpoke and Tuppence were on their way to work when Tuppence said, 'You know that nurse who calls herself Gail, which we now know is not her name? She hasn't been at work for the past two days, and no one has heard from her. So, if I were you, girls, I wouldn't be straying too far from my gun ...'

'Shit!' they said. 'We didn't come to get shot at.'

'I know,' said Tuppence, 'but it's better to be ready than dead.'

'Jesus,' said Slowpoke, 'did you have to put it that way?'

*   *   *

The manager of the retirement village who was calling himself Brian was beginning to worry, knowing the enemy had now lost one of their operatives and a crucial part of their merchandise of which he had, but couldn't read what it said. He needed to find if the store manager and his wife were who he thought they were. Although he knew she would not be his wife, she would be KGB, if that's who they were. He needed to let them know that he had the surgery instructions safe, if that's what this document was, and they needed to push on to obtain the rest of the merchandise before it was too late. Were there others he could trust, or was he the only one and the rest were his opponents from various countries? He was also concerned about the two blokes at the runway and the bloke who recently arrived at the treatment plant. He imagined that they all had known each other before they had arrived.

Osmar, or that's what he was calling himself, now had disposed of the body and had arrived in Eden, staying at the Twin Bays Motor Inn. He needed to make sure all was ready on the island before he committed himself. He decided to pick up the jet ski and visit the island to find out for himself.

Up until now, the KGB operatives were working independently. Each knew there were others on the island but not who they were, and each one was wondering where their help might come from if they needed it. Who were just ordinary island residents and who was the enemy? Then there was that group from the flats that always seemed to be together. Nothing really unusual about that but there was just something about them that was a red flag.

*   *   *

Slim and Wiggy had been curious for some time as to what might have been in the old shed next to the jetty with two railway lines running into the water. They were down at the boat today and their curiosity had got the better of them. There were no windows, and the steel door was padlocked with an expensive large padlock, which seemed overkill for a shed like that.

'There's got to be something in here that goes down into the water,' Slim said.

They decided to unscrew a corrugated panel off the back of the shed to get a look inside.

'Shit, look at those,' Wiggy said.

There were two, almost new, high-powered jet skis on roller frames to roll down the tracks into the water. There was a sticker on the side of them that said, 'Last Chance Island Village'.

'What would the old people in the retirement village want with these?' said Slim.

'You mean, old people like us,' Wiggy said. 'Well, I reckon you and I would have a ball on these things even at our age.'

They screwed the panel back on and drove back to the flats.

'I'm still not convinced these jet skis are for use by the retirees,' said Slim. 'Most of them look like they couldn't ride a three-wheeled bike, let alone a powerful jet ski.'

'Well, what do you think?'

'No idea, but I think we need to watch them closely and see what they're for.'

* * *

Felix had been instructed by Bruno, who had taken charge, to find out more about the group whose friendship seemed too good to be true and very unusual at the speed they had become friends. Because the school and the kindergarten were built as one, the teachers in both shared a lunchroom, and that's where Slowpoke and Auntie were now having coffee.

'Ahh, just the ladies I want to see,' Felix called out aggressively, as he came into the room. 'Why are you two wanting to work here on this isolated island?'

The two girls panicked as he came across threateningly, and Slowpoke fumbled inside her hessian bag for her gun. The safety catch was off. She pulled the trigger and shot a hole through the bag, shooting Felix in the foot. His cover had not been blown and if things went bad, he knew he would just kill them both. Slowpoke had probably saved their lives, although she didn't know it.

Felix hobbled next door to the hospital where another person in the same group was the nurse. He would need to be careful what he said, and he wouldn't be surprised if she also had a gun.

He said, 'That stupid woman at the school shot me.'

'Well, what did you expect?' she said. 'I heard you were very hostile and demanded to know why they were here. I would have shot you as well, and I'm a better shot than she is. Women working alone are entitled to protect themselves and a police report about this incident will be sent to Eden. Don't be a sook. You only have a flesh wound to the foot, which I will bandage.'

The incident was passed on to Wing Nut and the Colonel. As much as they would like to help, it was too early in the plan because their cover would be blown, and the merchandise had not been located yet. Did they think they could hold out or did they need to be extracted? Auntie and Slowpoke were all for being extracted immediately. Slim said the boys would keep a close watch on the girls at work from now on. One of them would be close by at all times. Nitro could drive back and forth in his buggy, Brewster could come and go on his Agi bike and either Wiggy or Slim would be available when the boat wasn't going out. It often did, to take people across for specialist appointments so they could return the same day, which was quite handy as it gave them a chance to link up with Wing Nut and the Colonel.

*   *   *

'Don't tell me you got shot by one of those frail women', Bruno said. 'Christ, that won't happen again. Next time, the Ferret can deal with it.'

Felix said, 'Yeah, well, just be careful of the one who shot me. You won't know where to stand. She shoots the bloody gun all over the place, and she doesn't know where it's going.'

The three men from The Syndicate had no idea that the Osmar who was coming was actually KGB. He could buy the merchandise with Iran's money and be gone in a flash, or he could kill the dark web members, take the merchandise and keep the money. They were all options to be considered at a later date. However, what he didn't know was that all the pieces of the merchandise were not together. There was still a piece missing, and he didn't know it was a KGB operative who had the missing piece. His part wouldn't come into play till all the merchandise was complete and the prearranged signal was received for delivery and money exchange, and where it was to take place.

The phony Osmar, who was now calling himself Gary, cruised into the jetty next to the boat that Slim and Wiggy were on.

Slim said, 'Now there's a shifty looking bloke, if ever I saw one.'

He had thick black curly hair and a short goatee beard on a well lived-in, hard looking face. He was thin but wiry and fit, somewhere around thirty, they guessed. You didn't have to be too smart to work out this bloke was bad news.

'Hello there,' he said, 'my name is Gary. The ferry isn't running, and I couldn't rent a boat, but this was a bit of fun anyway.'

'How can we help?' said Wiggy.

'I have come over to look at one of the flats I might buy as a holiday place for the family.'

'Follow the road round to the left, and you will see the flats and the agent's office on the corner,' said Slim.

They watched him jog up the road like a professional runner.

'Well,' said Wiggy, 'I reckon all the players are gathering. He's not here to buy a bloody flat and he doesn't look like a family man, either. He's definitely a new player in the game, so where does he fit in and whose side is he on? The only thing we know for sure is he's not on our side.'

* * *

Bruno said, 'It's time we sorted this shit heap out. I know for a fact the storekeepers are Russian, and Pham Linh was killed at the retirement village pool, so the odds on this so-called Brian being Russian is also good. I have heard him talking, and he has that European emphasis on his words. This has to be dealt with quickly before the buyer gets here.'

The Ferret said he could speak a little Russian so he would pay the storekeepers a visit to see if they were actually Russian.

* * *

Nikolai said to Annika, 'Brian from the retirement village swore in Russian today when getting his fuel, so I smiled back at him to acknowledge I knew what he had said. He said that I should check that the large potato bag wasn't open to the mice in the vegetable shed. I found this note in the bag.'

He read the note to her: 'We are now three under the same

flag. I have the surgical implant documents that Pham Linh had. She was an agent for The Syndicate on the dark web. The information on who she was was in a secret compartment on her bracelet along with the numbers 416. I have no idea what the numbers mean. The men working on the runway are not who they say they are, and neither is the one from the sewage plant. Invite me to dinner this week and we will formulate our plan.'

'Well,' said Annika, 'at least we know we have part of the merchandise, and the packages can't be sold without it.'

Brian was invited to dinner at the general store, and they were drinking vodka and discussing their next move when the front shop doorbell rang. Annika said she would see who it was. As she got closer, she could see through the glass door it was one of the men who were working on the runway. She thought he might have needed something after hours, although she was hesitant after hearing what Brian thought about them.

She opened the glass door and said, 'Yes, can I help you?'

He said, 'Cigarettes' in Russian.

She made a fatal mistake and answered in Russian. He shot her through the left eye, and as the gun was fitted with a silencer, it hardly made a noise.

'Why hasn't Annika come back yet?' Brian said.

They went to check and found her dead at the front door.

'We will get rid of the body,' said Nikolai, 'and tell everyone there was a death in the family and she has gone home. Not entirely untrue, is it, Brian? After all, she was KGB family, and as luck happens, the ferry is due tomorrow which she could have travelled on.'

Brian, alias Boris Sokolov, said, 'I have had an escape

plan for myself and any comrades who might require it if everything goes bust. I will take you there tonight', and he showed him a small transmitter hidden in a cupboard behind a false wall.

*   *   *

That night, Tuppence said, 'One of the patients at the hospital is too sick to stay here. She will need to go by boat to Eden. I know the ferry will be here tomorrow, but she is too sick for that, she will need to be put in a cabin on *Mystery*.'

Wiggy said, 'Slim and I will go down tonight and get the boat and the cabin ready for tomorrow.'

While they were below deck setting up the cabin, they heard the jet skis start up. They fired up *Mystery* and followed at a distance with no lights. Slim had the binoculars switched to night mode and could see them up ahead quite plainly. When the jet skis got to where the Herring Bone Strait meets the Pacific Ocean, they simply disappeared.

'Well, wherever they have gone, we don't want them to see us, so let's come back in daylight. We will have the boat out after taking the sick lady and Tuppence to hospital in Eden.'

*   *   *

Nikolai and Brian, as he was calling himself, had taken the jet skis up a narrow gap between the rocks just before the Herring Bone Strait got to the rough waters of the Pacific Ocean. The entrance to the cave was completely hidden by the overhang of the rocks. Tied up near the entrance was a fibreglass runabout with a 100 hp outboard motor. The cave was about thirty metres deep and had a small Honda generator and a long exhaust pipe running to the outside of the cave. The generator supplied the lighting for the cave and the transmitter radio, or anything requiring 240 volts.

They were met by a man called Zachery, a tall thin man with long hair and rimless glasses. He was softly spoken and could have easily been mistaken for a man of the cloth. There was a fold-out picnic table and a fold-out chair, a gas cooker and a small esky fridge. It had been made as comfortable as possible with a single camp stretcher.

'Hello, Zachery,' Brian said. 'This is Nikolai. I am showing him our exit plan in case anything happens to me.'

Zachery brought out the vodka and sat on the chair, the others on a rock ledge.

'How much longer do you think we will be here?' said Zachery.

'We have had a few setbacks, and we may even have to leave without the package. I will keep you informed via the radio. You might even have to leave by yourself in the boat. If we do get our hands on the package, we will be bringing it here for safety as planned.'

* * *

Wiggy and Slim arrived at Eden with Tuppence and the patient and used the opportunity to see Wing Nut. Wiggy spoke about the jet skis and where they went last night. It was suggested that they hire a jet ski and tow it back, as they didn't have an excuse to use the ones on the island. They hired a double seater jet ski for a week, and the Spiders could have a play with it if they wanted to.

The next day they took the jet ski and the boat to where they saw the jet skis disappear. As they slowly cruised past the rocks near the entrance to the ocean, they saw a small gap where the water was flowing through a split in the rocks, wide enough for a small boat or jet ski. They anchored the boat away from the entrance and fired up their jet ski. Very slowly and carefully, they crept up the small channel. At the same time they saw a cave entrance, a hailstorm of bullets came out of the cave. Wiggy was hit in the arm and a bullet had grazed Slim's shoulder.

They went back to the boat and got the rifle and two stun grenades, which deafen and stun you unconscious. This time they left the jet skis at the entrance and waded in. It was only waist deep. On a slight corner of the channel, there was a flat rock that gave them some cover, and they were able to see the entrance to the cave. Although they couldn't see him, they knew he would be watching and he had the advantage, or so he thought.

Slim clicked the stun grenade into the rifle attachment and fired it into the cave. Boom!

'Jesus,' he said, 'that was deafening.'

'Well, that was the idea, wasn't it?'

They waded further into the cave. A tall, thin man was lying on the ground, bleeding from one ear, compliments of the stun grenade. They sat him up against the cave wall and he slowly came to.

'Hello, china,' Wiggy said.

The man said, 'I'm not Chinese.'

'We know, you dick head. It means china plate, as in mate. You won't be alive long enough to use it. Who are you anyway?'

'I am Zachery, from Russia. I come here for holidays to fish.'

'Bullshit,' said Slim, 'Why do you need that transmitter over there?'

'I need for safety if I get sick.'

'That is also bullshit, Zachery, but good bullshit. So, before we shoot you and your boat, what are you doing here?'

'I told you, fishing.'

'No,' Wiggy said, 'wrong answer' and he shot him three times, once for his arm, once for Slim's shoulder and once for being a liar.

'Liar, liar, pants on fire, Russian,' Slim said. 'I think we should float the boat out to the jet skis, so we don't get wet again, and sink it in the entrance to block at least some of it. We will leave the Ruskie here to rot.'

They filled the boat and motor with holes and watched it sink.

Wiggy said, 'I think you would find Boris the retirement village manager at the other end of that transmitter.'

On their way back to the island, they rang Sparkie and gave her all the details to pass on to Wing Nut.

Chapter 4

Gary went first to the general store. He suspected that was where people gathered and gossiped, and that would be where the KGB would have set up a listening watch with its members. Otherwise, he would have to get his intel somewhere else. The location scanner that had been inserted into Osmar's body had stopped pinging, but the location device in the handle of the Gladstone bag was still pinging away normally at Eden. These signals were being relayed via global satellites back to a control centre deep on the edge of the Tabas salt lands in Iran. This information was then passed on to the high-ranking officials who were responsible for the procurement of the merchandise.

Back-up Plan B was at once implemented due to the amount of money that was involved and the importance of owning the merchandise. Taxi drivers Dimitri and Alexis were sharing a two-bedroom apartment in Carlton, a suburb of Melbourne, and they had been waiting for such a call. The message simply said, 'Your customer is ready to be picked up.'

*   *   *

The Spiders were now on full alert and carried their weapons with them wherever they went, and when they could, they went in pairs. The girls were always accompanied by one of the boys.

Wiggy said, 'I knew, when we were offered this bullshit, it wasn't going to be just listening and watching. We're not anywhere near experienced to handle what's going on here, or worse still, what's about to go down. We've been told we are on our bloody own and there are no police on the island.'

'No worries,' Brewster said. 'I may not be James Bond, but I've got my own set of gadgets.'

Wiggy said, 'The only set of gadgets you've got are in your pants and they're not going to be any good here. I'm just concerned we could get hung out to dry.'

*   *   *

Dimitri and Alexis knew the transaction was to take place on an island in Australia, and since the bag was pinging at Eden, it must be happening at Last Chance Island, which was just off the coast. Dimitri was a licensed fixed wing pilot, so they leased a Cessna 150, a two-seater aircraft, from a place at the Bairnsdale airport called 'Puddle Jumpers R Us'. The Cessna has a range of 700 kilometres and since the island they were flying to was only 280 kilometres away, it would also give them the opportunity to use the aircraft for the return trip.

They were told the island had a small landing strip, but they didn't know what condition it would be in, so it was advisable to do a fly past circuit first, and if not suitable, they could land back at Eden. There was no air traffic control on the island but there was a windsock. They flew low over the island and the strip looked okay to land on, so they flew back to Eden to follow the pinging of the bag before landing on the island.

The Syndicate men were checking that the steel cover over the trench was still in working condition when the Cessna flew low down the length of the runway. The wheels of the aircraft were only a few metres above the Ferret's head.

'Okay,' Bruno said, 'that's enough warning we need to get that document back today and send the signal for the transfer of the merchandise. Felix, go back to the hospital to get the dressing changed and make that bloody nurse talk. We need to start eliminating some of these players till we get the documents.'

Tuppence was busy catching up on the outpatient's paperwork at her desk, and Brewster was outside on the pretence of unblocking a drain. He saw the truck pull up and Felix get out with his bandaged foot, obviously to have the dressing changed, but Brewster would stay close just in case.

Felix sat opposite Tuppence, drew his Glock pistol and spoke.

'Right. No more Mr Nice Guy, nursing lady. I want to know who you all are.'

She didn't see what all the fuss is about. Everyone had come separately to take up advertised positions, she said, as she slowly unclipped the gun from its cradle under the desk and fired it. Because he was sitting opposite her, Felix was shot in the crutch, which didn't do the family jewels any good. Felix screamed in pain and dropped his Glock. Brewster heard the shot and appeared in the doorway. Felix was wriggling around in the chair in pain.

Brewster said, 'Look, we've had enough of this shit' and he shot him twice.

'Jesus,' Tuppence said, 'what do we do now?'

'We put him in his truck and push him and the truck over the cliff. You drive the truck, I'll follow on the Agi bike and you come back with me on the bike. If anyone asks, that bloke never came to the hospital today. And, by the way, Tuppence, is there some reason you girls can't shoot someone in a normal part of the body?'

'What does that mean?' she said.

'The count so far is a ceiling light, two holes in a handbag, a foot and a set of family jewels. I can't wait to see what's next.'

* * *

Gary had managed to link up with Nikolai and Brian and was brought up to date on who the likely players were. He knew that Brian had the documentation for the surgical instructions. The problem was that they didn't know who this other group was, who all seemed to be just a little bit too friendly but decided that they were to be left alone if possible. If they were anyone of concern, they would be Australian Government personnel, and there was no need to have them to worry about as well. They had enough on their plate.

Nitro was on his way to get the keys for the pool shed when he saw one of the runway workers leaving the pool area. He went into the retirement village office area and asked the receptionist for the keys to the pool shed, but she had already given the keys to someone else a half an hour ago, who said he was meeting the manager there. Nitro knew that meant the manager, Brian, was probably dead. When Nitro opened the pool shed, sure enough, there was Brian, eyes bulging, tongue hanging out, swinging from the ceiling rafters. A chair had been pushed over to make it look like a suicide, and an empty compendium was lying on the floor, so whatever had been in there was now in the possession of the runway workers, whoever they were. Nitro decided to lock the door and keep the keys and what he had found until tomorrow.

* * *

Dimitri and Alexis had followed the pinging to the Twin Bays Motor Inn. The door of room number 416, the same numbers on Pham Linh's bracelet, was easily opened and the Gladstone bag was found in the wardrobe. They had been in possession of the code for the bag from Iran before they left. In the bag were the three cheques, several passports and the signal for the arrival to pay for the merchandise. When and how it would happen would be done in an arranged coded message.

Dimitri and Alexis would fly on to the island, make the change and fly off again. They couldn't believe how easy this was going to be. The signal was sent and received by the two operatives from The Syndicate workers on the runway, and the exchange would take place tomorrow at 4.30 pm.

The Spiders had, by this time, realised that the air strip would be an important part of the the chips and their movement. Nitro and Brewster had been on a daylight shift to monitor any action at the runway. On the next morning's watching shift, there was a lot of action at the runway. The Ferret had opened the steel plate across the trench and removed a steel box. The steel cover plate across the trench had been closed but swivelled sideways inside the pit. The one calling himself Bruno had arrived and was assembling some sort of machinery that they had earlier hidden in the small shed. He said to the Ferret, with the truck and Felix missing, it was just as well the transfer was taking place now. Nitro decided it was time to alert the Spiders that something was about to happen.

They used the radio to pass on the intel to Wing Nut. The only answer they got back was 'Roger that.'

'Shit,' Wiggy said, 'I think Slim and I should go back with the girls and go to the boat. Nitro, you go back to the runway to keep us informed and Brewster, you go and break open the shed with the jet skis. Fire one up and bring it over to the side of the boat.'

The radio squawked with the message: 'Imperative you follow trail if transfer takes place. Authorities will be your support when required.'

'Yeah, bullshit,' said Wiggy, 'just like they've been so far. Where have the police been with all these murders?'

Slim said, 'I think, apart from the first murder of the store managers, our secret service has stood the police down for fear of jeopardising the mission, so we're on our own till they decide otherwise.'

*　*　*

Nikolai and Gary, a KGB operative like Nikolai, decided, once they heard the village manager had been killed and his part of the merchandise was gone, it was time for them to leave. Osmar thought he still had the money so not all was lost. The ferry was due in the morning. They would retrieve the money and be gone.

The ferry docked at the island at 8 am, unloaded the stores and took on the passengers for Eden, including the two Russians. The jet ski that Gary came over with was being towed behind the ferry with the one the Spiders had hired. When they returned to the motel and found the door was open, they drew their guns and entered the room. It had been stripped and searched, and the Gladstone bag was gone.

'Shit!' Gary said. 'We've got to get back to the island. Someone else has been here and they will be on the island now with the money.'

The two of them jumped back on the jet ski and headed back.

*   *   *

Dimitri and Alexis were on the final approach to the island runway. Bruno and the Ferret were behind the small shed, with the remote control for the steel plate, when the wheels of the Cessna 150 touched the runway halfway down. The steel plate rose up out of the trench two feet high.

'Jesus, what's that?' said Alexis.

They didn't stand a chance. The wheels of the Cessna hit the steel plate at a 100 km/h, the aircraft flipped into the air and slid down the runway upside down. Bruno and the Ferret looked into the cockpit at the two men who were dead. Just to make sure, they pumped two bullets into each of them, took the bag with the bank cheques and passports and set fire to the plane.

Behind the small shed was what Bruno had been putting together, a two-person ultralight trike with a small engine. It only needed sixty metres to take off and fifty metres to land and could cruise at a hundred kilometres per hour for seventy kilometres or eighty kilometres per hour for a hundred and thirty kilometres. They got ready to push it onto the runway.

Nitro had made the phone call to the boat and was on his way to the jetty in his electric cart. Brewster was at the boat with one of the jet skis. When Nitro arrived and they were all on board, they were backing away from the jetty when they heard the ultralight start up. Bruno was the pilot, with the Ferret sitting in the rear seat. They reached the lift-off speed at sixty kilometres per hour and were airborne over the bay area. Wiggy pushed the big cruiser's twin control levers forward and the twin 600 horsepower Caterpillar engines answered the call.

As they left the jetty, the jet ski with the two Russians arrived. They saw the shed was open and one jet ski was still in there. Nikolai jumped off the back of the jet ski and onto the one in the shed, and they both sped off after the boat and the ultralight.

Bruno said to the Ferret, 'That's the island's cruiser down there. They must be taking the guests on an afternoon run … and look, they also have the jet skis out.'

Brewster was travelling on his jet ski behind the cruiser in its wash. Nitro and Slim pointed to him to look back behind at the two jet skis that were coming up fast. He waved an acknowledgement and spun out of the wash and back to check who they were. As he got closer, he started taking on gun fire from the two jet skis; one round whistled past his head and another embedded itself in the seat behind him. He recognised Nikolai but he had no idea who the other one was. He spun away back to the boat, came alongside and told them who it was. Guns were drawn, Slim grabbed the Sig Sauer with a fourteen-round magazine, and when they saw Auntie and Slowpoke getting their weapons out of their bags, everyone hid in the cabin.

The ultralight had swung around to check who was in the boat. As they passed over the two jet skis, they were fired upon.

'That's Nikolai from the store,' the Ferret said, 'I don't know the other one, but the ones in the boat are that group we've been trying to find out who they are. I recognise the nurse from the hospital and the one on the jet ski is supposedly the island plumber we spoke to that day we were digging the trench.'

Bruno said, 'We need to take as many of them out while we're still in Herring Bone Strait.'

The cruiser was now taking fire from above and from the jet skis. Brewster had been told by Slim that the second ski was probably the bloke who called himself Gary.

Brewster rode back to the boat and called out to Wiggy, 'Throttle off to a slow speed and let me see if I can get a jet ski to follow me to cross in front of the boat. You do the rest.'

Brewster wove in and out between the jet skis, firing and ducking. He slowed right down as if he had been hit and slumped across the steering. One of the jet skis followed him for the kill, as the group on the boat could only watch and hope this might work. Brewster limped the ski slowly across in front of the boat which was now just virtually idling. When Nikolai made the mistake of crossing in front of the cruiser, Brewster gunned his jet ski and Nikolai was caught off guard. Wiggy pushed the twin levers all the way home, the big 600 horsepower twin Caterpillar engines reared the boat up over the top of Nikolai's jet ski and the shaft-driven propellers tore a huge hole in Nikolai's stomach with his intestines trailing out into the bay.

Slim said to the girls, 'Start firing at that flying bicycle thing. It doesn't matter if you don't hit it. It might scare them to keep their distance.'

So they started firing at the trike, which was more manoeuvrable than the boat. Slowpoke just managed to put a new magazine on the pistol without any damage to anyone or anything and open-fired just as Wiggy swung the boat hard around. Bullets from Slowpoke's gun went everywhere in the sky, and something fell into the boat. They saw the Ferret grab his head.

'What's that that fell in here?' Slim said, as he picked it up. 'Well, bugger me, Slowpoke. You've just shot the Ferret's ear off.'

Even in the midst of what was happening, they had to have a bloody laugh.

'Wait till Brewster finds out – he was waiting to see what you might hit next. If you can somehow hit them between the foot and the ear, you will make us all happy,' they said.

Gary was determined to get the money back, but he didn't know who actually had it. He suspected the ones on the flying bike, but the boat people were a hindrance, a bloody annoyance. The hang glider ultralight dropped its height over Gary's jet ski and the Ferret, holding his head where his ear used to be, filled Gary's body with bullets.

They were coming up to the entrance to the Pacific Ocean. The hang glider had twice the speed the cruiser had, so the distance between them was ever widening, but Brewster's jet ski was managing to keep the distance equal. As they crossed the rough water into the Pacific Ocean and the ultralight along with Brewster on the jet ski were almost out of sight, a Robinson R44 helicopter appeared and hovered where the ultralight had put down into the ocean. They hovered just a few feet above the water, and the Ferret with one ear and Bruno climbed in. Brewster was turning his jet ski around to go back when a larger helicopter came from over the top of the cliffs, a Chinook Tiger Attack 15 EC135. It hovered right next to Brewster.

A voice yelled, 'Hello, code name Brewster, I'm Lieutenant Commander Harrigan with the Australian Secret Intelligence Service and I have been on the island for several months, waiting for the transaction. The Colonel and Wing Nut have kept me up to date with all your surveillance reports. We have a tracking device fitted to the Robinson R44 so we'll know where it's going. I have a radio call for you from the Colonel that you can take in the cockpit.'

'Hello, Brewster, do you copy?'

'Copy,' said Brewster.

'What a marvellous job your group has done! I would have hated to come up against your group in your younger days. I hear your calling yourself the Spiders of Spy – what a classic. I have just this minute spoken to your group in the cruiser on the boat's radio frequency and congratulated them on a job well done. We would like you to continue your undercover work for us, but only if you agree. I would admit it's been rougher than we expected for operatives of your ages, but you have performed like professionals and that's why you're being asked to continue tracking the FLCs and their packages. Your groups have said, it's all in or no one's in, so now it's up to you, Brewster. Auntie, your other half, was more concerned about whether the neighbours had fed the goldfish. We want to get you in somehow as a stool pigeon if we can. What do you say?'

'Shit,' said Brewster. 'I've always considered myself as a pretty nice bloke. Now you're asking me to be a stool pigeon. I don't think I could identify with that role.'

'Don't worry. Your unassuming manner along with your manly skills and talkative personality will be perfect, so what do you say?'

'Well I don't actually get a say, do I? The others are in, so I guess, one in, all in – but only if you give the girls some real serious training with their 9 mm pistols. They have to stop putting the guns in their bloody handbags. You need to give them some sort of an under-skirt holster, purely for our safety. So, what happens now?'

Harrigan said, 'We now know we are dealing with a worldwide crime ring known as The Syndicate. These chips will undoubtedly be going somewhere in Europe to be sold again to the highest bidder. You, Brewster, will be sent there by yourself. The Spiders, as you call yourself, will be sent to join you afterwards when we have established your stool pigeon infiltration role, and then you will all be, with each other's support again, at a location that will soon become apparent.'

'Those two, Bruno and the Ferret, know who I am.'

The Syndicate never use the same agents twice after a mission. Those two will be disposed of on their return. This mission will not be seen as a failure because they still have the FLCs and the Iranian money, which will be hidden somewhere in their world banking system and money laundering circles. They have lost four of their members on this mission: Mavis and Bert, the store managers found at the bottom of the cliff; Pham Linh, the cleaner drowned in the pool; and Felix who was shot by Tuppence and Brewster at the hospital. The Russians have also lost five of their KGB agents: the second store managers Annika, shot at the store by the Ferret and Nikolai killed on the jet ski; Boris Sokolov, the retirement village manager hung by Bruno and Gary, alias Osmar, alias who knows, shot by the Ferret from the ultra light; and the nurse, Galina Soloyova, shot by the Ferret on the runway. The Iranians didn't do any better. They lost three of their agents: the original Osmar shot outside Cann River by the driver Gary; and Dimitri and Alexis killed in the plane crash on the runway. These agents are seen as expendable items, cannon fodder, part of the cost of a mission, and you can bet the Iranians will be chasing their $250 million. They won't let that go unchallenged.'

Back on the cruiser, Wiggy said, 'It's a bloody miracle at our age we haven't had a heart attack or been shot in the arse by one of these girls. I think we should go back to Fairview, treat ourselves to a lobster dinner at the Lobster Rock Restaurant and wait for the call for part two. Remember what the Colonel said: make sure your passport is up to date and current for at least six months. And I told you, Slim, and Brewster not to do any macho hero stuff on this trip. I'm surprised you're not there with him wherever he is going.'

Auntie said, 'I'll probably never see the lovable fool again.'

'Yes, you will. We will see him when we join him, wherever that will be,' Slim said.

Chapter 5

Brewster had been given a new passport and a backpack with a set of clothes and toiletries. He was loaded onto a military C130 Hercules aircraft and flown to London for a briefing with Scotland Yard and the UK's secret intelligence service, MI6.

The British agent who was running the briefing said, 'If you're wondering why we are using an ordinary civilian, Brewster, agencies all over the world with sophisticated methods and intel can detect infiltrated agents in their network almost instantly, which amounts to a dead agent. So, we use selected civilian counteragents who usually are not detected until the information we need is gathered.'

Brewster said, 'So, when they detect me after you get what you want, I'll be dead – is that how it works?'

'The part you and your friends will play in this is of the utmost importance. The Orient Express leaves Paris in two days' time on a five-day trip to Istanbul. There will be a woman on the train called Lola. She will get on in Paris and will be in possession of one part of the merchandise. Which part, we don't know. We need you to befriend her, win her confidence and get that information for us. You will be boarding the train in Paris also. Be very careful – she may look like a lovely woman, but she is one of The Syndicate's top agents, a trusted courier of important merchandise, who has successfully carried out many missions with many kills to her name, most of them said to be during or before a sex act where she entices her victims to her bedroom for the kill.

'The cost of cabins on the Orient Express from Paris is 34,000 pounds, so to save on cost, the rest of your group will be getting on at Budapest with their cabins booked through to Istanbul. Lola will most certainly be travelling with two support agents, so your group will need to be very careful. We need to get this information without a fuss if we can.'

* * *

Back at Fairview, the Spiders had been given the green light for travel to London and then on to Budapest. They were given a briefing by the Colonel and Wing Nut prior to leaving. They travelled to London with Qantas and then three hours flying time with Lufthansa to Budapest from where they would board the Orient Express bound for Istanbul and hopefully a secret link up with Brewster. Auntie and Slowpoke had been given extensive training at the pistol range and were now fair shots. Special girdle holsters had been designed for them, and their skirts and dresses all had side zips on where the gun was for quick and easy access – which made everyone feel safer! Their guns had been taken from them and would be given back to them in Budapest by MI6 and ASIO.

The girls were excited about going on the Orient Express until Slim and Nitro reminded them this trip would be far more dangerous than the last one.

Wiggy said, 'I don't think they care how bloody old we are. If it all goes wrong, no one will ever know who was responsible for the balls-up. Politicians and government officials will pass the buck around until it all just goes away. And like I have said before, we could all be hung out to dry. Anyway, we're in it up to our neck now and our lives could very well be on the line, so get those holiday thoughts out of your minds and watch each other's backs – and don't go anywhere without your weapons. Good luck to all of us old pricks!'

* * *

Brewster boarded the train in Paris as planned and was shown to cabin number 14 by the butler. The cabins were magnificent with ornate finishes and intricate detailing. In fact, the whole train was unbelievable – you could have easily been back on the train on 4 October 1883 for its first journey. Brewster set about checking where everything was: the emergency exit doorways, passageways and toilets, dining car and club lounge car, emergency stop devices, staff quarters and luggage car.

Lola and her henchmen were probably already on the train, so the cat and the mouse would soon meet. A cloth holster was sewn into the back of his pants so there was no telltale bulge in his jacket. He couldn't afford any mistakes when dealing with Lola. She would be very experienced in detecting any signs of danger or actions that would blow his cover.

You can never be overdressed on the Orient Express; formal evening attire is required for dinner, a jacket and tie for lunch was required and smart day wear at all other times. Women wear their most glamorous clothes and stylish cocktail dresses and the latest fashionable hats. He watched the alluring woman walk into the dining car. Her beauty was hard to ignore. The woman was simply stunning, her features were flawless. He had seen photos of her at MI6, but they were nothing like the real thing.

He sat at an opposite table, and she acknowledged him with a smile and after the meal, invited him to her table for a drink, which surprised him. She was beautiful but arrogant, cold-hearted and someone not to be trusted. He wondered if she somehow already knew who he was, but the game was definitely now on.

'So, what brings a lady on the Orient Express by herself?'

'Oh, I'm not by myself. I work as a courier for a diamond company, so I never travel alone.'

She introduced herself as Lola and said she was going to Turkey to repay a debt and asked him where he was going. He introduced himself as Brewster and said he was a retired race driver and was simply holidaying till he decided what he would do next.

'A race car driver? How exciting! I think the company I work for might be interested in your expertise. I'll give you my card in the morning.'

Brewster said good night and as he left the dining car, he spotted them. Even though they were immaculately dressed, they were hard to miss. One of them had a permanent smile on his face from a scar that ran across his lips, his offsider had thick red hair and a large square jaw, and both of them had that familiar bulge in their jackets.

Back in his cabin, he wondered how much Lola actually knew, or maybe he was just imagining it. He would need to be very, very careful with this woman. The rest of the Spiders would be coming on board at Budapest tomorrow and he was looking forward to seeing Auntie and the gang, but they would have to be careful how they connected with each other on the train.

* * *

On board, the girls were ecstatic about the train and couldn't believe they were travelling on the famous Orient Express. Brewster had managed to catch up with Nitro and Slim in the passage and while Wiggy and the girls kept watch, he brought them up to date with Lola and her henchmen. Nitro and Slim had now seen the henchmen and were quick to nickname them Blood Nut and Jaws. The Spiders' job was to deal with the henchmen so that Brewster only had Lola to deal with, but even without her henchmen's support, she would still be a handful.

Slim had done a reconnaissance of the train and found the release switch for the emergency doors in each of the carriages. Auntie and Slowpoke were busy changing into cocktail dresses for drinks in the club car and then lunch. Sparkie was assembling their small satellite phone in the girls' cabin, as there was no normal phone reception now until Istanbul, then she would join the others in the dining car for lunch. She had opted for a flowing mini dress with a statement sleeve and a soft hue of cadmium red.

* * *

The American 'eye in the sky' satellite intel and agents buried deep in Russia suggested that they had not given up on the FLCs, and the way things were in Russia, it was really only speculation on what their position would be with the merchandise. The government of the Federation of Russia had been in secret discussions with the KGB chairman and his six deputies to ascertain what intel they had on where these chips might be located at the moment.

The deputies said, 'We believe the FLCs are on their way to Iran in exchange for the Iran money that The Syndicate has taken.'

The KGB believed The Syndicate weren't keen on the possibility of the Iranians pursuing them over the money for years to come.'

'It just wouldn't be worth it,' the KGB Chairman said, 'so we believe they are on their way from Rome to Turkey or somewhere close by.'

And if the truth was known, the KGB would already have an agent on site somewhere. They weren't in the habit of advertising their plans.

* * *

When the Spiders entered the dining car for lunch, Brewster was sitting with Lola looking quite relaxed, which didn't impress Auntie. She raised her eyebrows as she walked past. Unknown to the group, their cabin butler was entering their cabins to search for anything he could find to indicate who they all were, and if they were in fact just tourists.

Nitro had left a cotton thread across the doorway, so he knew someone had been in there. Slowpoke entered their cabin and found Jaws pointing a gun at her. He pushed her at gunpoint down the passage to the emergency door at the end of the carriage. She was facing him with her back to the door and he had his back to the passageway when Nitro smacked him across the head, allowing Slowpoke to move from the door as Jaws fell against it. Slim arrived, reached into the control box and opened the emergency door, and out went Jaws.

'Thank you, both of you,' she said. 'That's a debt I will never be able to repay.'

Tonight would be the last night on the train and the girls would be dressing up for the occasion. Sparkie decided not to go to dinner. Considering what had happened with Jaws, and that someone might search their cabins again, it might be her turn for some excitement. The girls were looking quite dapper. Tuppence wore a stunning, mermaid silhouette, long evening gown with intricate lace and an open back with an eye-catching neckline, a clutch bag and silver and gold heels. Her gun was concealed in a false chiffon hem in the front of the gown. Slowpoke wore a long chiffon halter-neck dress with long sleeves and a black and scarlet elegant print down one side which had a concealed zipper gun compartment, silver fleet court shoes and a scarlet matching clutch bag. Auntie decided on a deep mauve, stylish jumpsuit of taffeta fabric with flared bottoms, matching high heeled shoes and a woven shoulder bag. The gun zipper on the side of the jumpsuit was disguised as a pocket.

Except for Sparkie back at the cabin and Brewster who was sitting with Lola, they were all together on a table for six. Blood Nut was looking lonely and pissed off by himself as he was unable to find his offsider – even though the Spiders had hung a sign on Jaw's cabin door that said, 'Do not disturb, passenger sick' – and so was Auntie, considering Brewster looked like he was enjoying himself just a bit more than he needed to. The dining car was full, and the soft murmur of conversation mixed with the soft dining music was quite relaxing.

Suddenly everything went black, and the soft music was replaced with gunfire and screaming. The Spiders hit the floor behind the table, guns drawn. There were red tracer rounds lighting up the room searching for their target. Nitro caught a glimpse of their cabin butler firing at them from the entrance, someone else was firing from the kitchen and Lola and Brewster were firing at both ends of the room. It sounded and felt like everyone in the dining car had a bloody gun; nobody really knew who was firing at whom.

Wiggy called out, 'The butler on the left and Blood Nut on the right, they're your targets.'

They sent a barrage of firepower left and right but when the stewards got the lights back on, they were both gone. There was blood on the floor where Blood Nut had been hit and a trail of blood went out through the kitchen area. Lola had been hit in the shoulder.

She handed Brewster a package while she checked her wound and said, 'Those three items are the jewels that I am carrying for my company. They are worth more than your life. Hold on to them while I dress my shoulder.'

Brewster now had the information he was sent to get, but things had got a lot more complicated.

Auntie had a flesh wound to her elbow and Wiggy had a bruised left testicle where the table had crashed down on his crutch in the dark. They were all told they would be interviewed by the authorities when the train got into Istanbul tomorrow. Nitro and Wiggy went after the butler and Slim followed the blood trail through the kitchen.

'There he goes, down the passageway,' Wiggy said.

As they went past Sparkie's door, she jumped out and fired at the butler, frightening buggery out of the two of them. When they got to the emergency door, it was open and the butler was climbing the steel external ladder on the side of the carriage.

Nitro said, 'I'll go after him, Wiggy.'

'I know you will. At eighty, I'm not going anywhere out there, not even if the train was stationary.'

Nitro climbed the ladder on to the roof. It was freezing cold and blowing a gale. Three bullet rounds whizzed past his head. The butler was now down between the carriages for protection while Nitro was exposed on top of the carriage. He had to lie flat for some protection from both the wind and the bullets. *This isn't going to work*, he thought, so he climbed back down to the ladder and called out to Wiggy.

'Go back two carriages and come up behind the butler. It's the only way to get to him. You'll just have to put your big girl pants on and go up the ladder. He needs to see that I'm still here. I'll keep firing a shot every now and then to keep him there.'

Jesus, Wiggy said to himself, eighty years old and I'm suddenly in the bloody circus!

He ran along two carriages, opened the emergency door and made hard work of climbing the steel ladder. He carefully stuck his head up and sure enough the butler was two metres away, firing at Nitro. Two well-aimed shots to the back of his head, and they watched the butler spiralling off the train into the countryside.

Slim wasn't as productive. He had followed the blood trail

back to what was obviously Blood Nut's cabin. He would be in there, tending to his wounds, or maybe he was dead, depending on where he had been shot.

The Spiders were all in Sparkie and Nitro's cabin for a debriefing when the sat phone red light started flashing. Sparkie answered it and put it on speaker. The bigwig from MI6 was on the other end. Brewster passed on what he had learnt from Lola.

The bigwig said, 'Most of the puzzle has unravelled now, so here is what we know. The Syndicate has decided to hand over the FLC merchandise, seeing they also have Iran's money, rather than having to watch their back for years to come. I suppose there's got to be some honour among thieves. So, here's what we think is going down. Lola will be the go-between for The Syndicate and the Iranians. Russia also want the FLC merchandise so they will be an issue for Lola and you.'

'Well, I would have thought we have done our bit, but you seem to be intent on getting us killed,' Slim said. 'We should have signed a contract for a huge amount of money to go to our family. We'll be lucky if the government pay the bloody funeral costs, if I know anything.'

'We are very lucky to have you people on board. Thank you.'

The radio went dead, and he was gone.

The Orient Express arrived at the beautiful Sırkecı railway station in Istanbul at 11.30 am amid much fuss and excitement. After everyone who had been in the dining car during the shooting was interviewed and had their names checked through Interpol, they were allowed to disembark from the train. This was going to be the most dangerous part of the mission. the perfect end would be that the FLC merchandise was handed over to MI6 for safekeeping, but that would be easier said than done.

Going through security checkout with a weapon if you had a permit was no problem. A vast amount of people in Turkey carried a weapon of some sort. Brewster was still operating independently from the group so he couldn't be seen with them in public, and who knows who else was out there watching? He wondered where Lola would have decided to make the switch. She would choose somewhere safe but not isolated. She was just up ahead so he spoke to her and asked how her shoulder was.

'Fine, thanks. This is Gus, one of my security guards. I don't think you've met him. He was also shot during the skirmish last night protecting the jewels that are very important to me.'

The Spiders knew Gus as Blood Nut.

Brewster said, 'I have my own set of family jewels that are also very important to me.'

He saw her smile for the first time since he had met her.

He said, 'I thought you had two guards.'

'Yes,' she said, 'He somehow got left at the station at Budapest. He should be here tomorrow.'

Well, that wasn't going to happen, not with Jaws lying somewhere on the side of the train line between Budapest and Istanbul.

Brewster asked Lola if she knew where he could buy some fresh clothes.

'Go to the Grand Bazaar, They have four thousand stalls to choose from. Whenever I come to Turkey, I always pay the bazaar a visit.'

Suddenly it dawned on Brewster that that would be

where the handover would take place. It was protected by thousands of people, had plenty of cover and you could easily lose yourself in the crowd.

The Spiders were all staying at the Mandarin Oriental Bosphorus Hotel, and that's where Brewster was now discussing plans for the bazaar tomorrow. The plan was to split into pairs and move through the bazaar separately from the other pairs. Wiggy would link up again with Tuppence, the others in their husband-and-wife teams.

'Use your phones to contact each other with your location if you have to. Remember, although we are in pairs, we will still have the support of each other.'

Chapter 6

Three Russians flew into Istanbul's smaller airport, Sibiha Gökcen Airport, on the Asian side. Both airports were quite a way from the city. The three knew this would be the last chance to grab the FLC package before it got into Iran, when all bets would be off.

The Butcher of Belarus was a psychopathic killer who cut his victims up just for the fun of it. He should have been disposed of at birth. Evil isn't born; it's made in the brain of the killer. The other two were simply KGB hitmen, and to them, it was just business as usual. They had a current photo of Lola, and they gambled that the bazaar would be where the exchange would take place. They would be there watching for her.

Lola had established contact with the two Iranian agents and the package would be handed over on hearing the designated password. It would take place at a particular clothing stall at the bazaar tomorrow. The Syndicate had been very explicit – the FLC package was to get into no one's hands but the Iranians, or she would pay with her life.

'So, I need everything to go like clockwork tomorrow,' she said to Gus.

It was unique as all the players were spread around

and about the front entrance of the bazaar, trying to look inconspicuous, and no one knew who each of them was, yet they were all there for the same reason, watching for Lola to arrive with the goodies along with whoever else she might have attracted.

At 11.30 am, a yellow taxi pulled up. Lola and Gus jumped out and went into the Grand Bazaar. Gus still had his arm in a sling and as he walked past Slim, part of a revolver could be seen resting in the sling. The Spiders dispersed into the bazaar with silencers fitted to their guns.

Gus and Lola suddenly split up. Nitro and Sparkie followed Gus who looked like he was just shopping. Slim and Slowpoke continued to tail Lola who also looked like she was just shopping and in no apparent hurry. The remainder of the group just circled around at a distance keeping watch. That's when they noticed the three suspicious looking characters. One of them had caught up with Gus and was tailing him; the other two were definitely following Lola. Slim rang Nitro who said yes, they had seen him and were on to him.

Lola had gone into a stall among one of the many racks of dresses. The Russian followed her in, and so did Slowpoke. The Russian was about to shoot Lola on the other side of the clothing rack when Slowpoke fired two shots. The first one went through the left breast of the female plastic mannequin, and the second hit the Russian in the face and he fell in among the long dresses. Slim heard the pop of the gun's silencer and hurried into the stall.

Slowpoke said, 'What are we going to do with him, so his slimy offsider doesn't find him?'

Slim said, 'Take a coathanger off one of those dresses and help me lift him up.'

They put the coathanger in the shoulders of his jacket and hooked the coathanger on the rack among the dresses. The rack was the perfect height with the coathanger to keep the dead Russian standing up hidden among the dresses. They casually walked out the other side of the stall and watched the other Russian looking for his mate. He came out of the stalls, shaking his head, and walked off. Lola also walked off, oblivious that she should have been dead and the FLC package gone.

Nitro and Sparkie were trailing some distance back from the Russian they were following. It was the Butcher of Belarus, and he was as cunning as a shithouse rat.

Gus had been aware that every time he looked back, the same three people seemed to be in the vicinity. He ducked into a candy stall and through into a leather belt stall, the back entrance of which led to a stall with birds and cages. Lola was waiting for him as this was the transfer stall for the FLC package.

She saw what was about to happen. The Butcher was coming round behind Sparkie and Nitro, and before anyone could stop him, he had driven a 33 cm Shiv into Sparkie's left ribs, puncturing her spleen. Lola had no idea who Nitro and Sparkie were, so she opened fire on the Butcher. She knew he was really after her. Gus was some distance away to cover their escape route if they had handed over the FLC package.

'Stay with me, Sparkie!' Nitro was telling Sparkie. 'Don't close your eyes. Stay awake, talk to me. Help is coming.'

The Turkish police and an ambulance arrived and transported Sparkie and Nitro to the Medical Park Göztepe Hospital and the authorities notified the embassy in London.

A military medical evacuation was initiated for Sparkie and Nitro back to Australia.

The Spiders now had a new purpose in life, a bigger one than the one they were sent here for as far as they were concerned.

* * *

The Iranian agents had watched the action unfold and were unwilling to try and make the switch of the FLC package at the moment under the circumstances. They were now aware of two foreign agents, almost certainly Russian, here on site, but they had no idea who the other people were, so the original plans would need to change.

The Spiders, who were now six, to keep their humour up were considering calling themselves the Silent Six and would be hell-bent on evening up the score.

'Jesus,' Wiggy said, 'you people forget how old and how unfit we all are. Don't get carried away. We have been very lucky so far. These people we are dealing with are bloody professionals, and you two', pointing to Auntie and Slowpoke, 'don't go near that bastard with the Shiv. Stay close to your opposite number at all times.'

Lola sent Gus to liaise with the Iranians. He spoke to them among the racks of clothing and informed them a message would be left at the birdcage stall tomorrow, where the handover would now take place.

The two Russians and Slim and Slowpoke were following Lola wherever she went, and they followed her to the booking office of the Mediterranean Shipping Company. She had taken care to ensure everyone knew where she was going and what she was doing. She was finally sick and tired of worrying about these pimps and thieves. They were all part of the same snake, just different ends, but one end could bite twice. If you want peace, you prepare for war.

She was going to eliminate the problem, but she needed suitable premises and the time to do it. Lola was going to send the FLC package via registered mail from the Central Post Office in Sırkeci to the Torcello Island Post Office in Venice, Italy. She had booked two single cabins for the four-day boat trip to Venice. That way, Lola could concentrate on eliminating the pests and not worry about the security of the package.

The Spiders called MI6 to enquire as to where the ship was going. After the initial toing and froing, MI6 eventually booked three double cabins with Oceania Cruisers. The Russians had done the same, which was what Lola was counting on. Lola had no idea who the others were. She had seen them on the train but put them down as tourists. Brewster had kept away from her, so she had no idea where he was or that he had anything to do with the so-called tourists.

As luck happened, they were on a different deck from Lola, Gus and the Russians, which gave them some freedom on their deck. They weren't aware that the FLC package wasn't on board, and neither were the Russians. On the second night out, Lola decided it was time for the routine she called 'seduction by death' and the Butcher would be first. She despised the way he had knifed that innocent woman at the bazaar. God wouldn't be fixing this; he would be sitting this one out.

She walked past the Butcher's table and asked him if he would like some company. He, of course, said yes, so Lola sat down. He was a really ugly bastard with stained yellow teeth.

His fingernails were bitten down to the quick and his breath stunk. She didn't mind; she wasn't going to be with him long.

After the meal, the Butcher made the mistake of inviting Lola back to his cabin.

She said, 'Thanks. That would be nice.'

He poured her a wine and they went out onto his balcony. She dropped the glass, and it broke. She picked up a large broken piece, and he said he would get another glass. Lola said, 'No need to bother' and rammed the broken glass into the artery in his neck. To stem the flow of blood which was pumping out through his fingers, she told him to lean over the railing to slow the flow and when he did, she pushed him over into the sea. It was a very dark night so nobody saw him go over. Lola cleaned up the blood from the balcony and left a note in his cabin that said, 'Staying with a lady friend in her cabin. Please make up the room. I may or may not come back. Money on the table for you.'

That left only one more Russian. She would sleep on how to dispose of him. There were still two day's travel, plenty of time.

Gus was becoming suspicious about the group they thought were tourists. He was sure he had seen at least one of them on the train and again at the bazaar. Although not unusual as they were in all the places you would expect to find tourists, he thought he had seen one of them again on the ship. Were they just tourists on their way to Venice or were they people to be concerned about? He wasn't sure, but he would treat them with caution and tell Lola his concerns.

The trick to all of this was not to leave a dead body on the ship to be discovered and raise the alarm, so Lola needed a plan that included the removal of the next Russian's body after the kill. Several possibilities were discussed with Gus. It was decided the simplest way was to just shoot him. They waited till he would be asleep around midnight and knocked on his cabin door. When he opened the door, they shot him in the head, wheeled his body in the laundry trolley to the stern of the ship and slid his body over, where the big twin propellers would suck him under and churn his body to nothing.

The ship docked at Venice's Stazione Maritime Station the next morning. Lola and Gus took a taxi to the Hotel Abbazia, about a hundred metres from the Santa Lucia train station. The Spiders were staying at the Hotel Guerrini in Lista di Spagne, about four hundred metres from the Santa Lucia station. Lola sent Gus to let the Iranians know they would be on the hop-on hop-off boat at 11 am going to Torcello Island.

Gus had noticed he was being followed by two of the so-called tourists, so he led them to the train station and on to the busy platform. Wiggy and Tuppence realised they had been had and took the necessary action. Once they were on the platform, it was easy to see what he was up too. Wiggy told Tuppence to stand among the crowd at the edge of the platform and be ready to quickly move to one side when he said, 'Now!' Wiggy was in the crowd behind Gus, who was moving up behind Tuppence. They heard the train's horn signalling it was coming into the station. As Gus raised his hands to push Tuppence onto the track, Wiggy called out, 'Now!' Tuppence moved to one side, and Wiggy pushed Gus off in front of the train, then they both disappeared into the crowd.

The next day, there was no sign of Gus, so Lola left without him. He knew where she was going and he would catch up, if he wasn't already dead. It was too risky to catch the same hop-on hop-off boat as Lola, so the Spiders caught the ferry five minutes later, and two Islamic looking men got on as well.

'I don't like the look of those two,' Slowpoke said.

'Well, don't keep staring at them,' Slim told her.

Lola had been to the post office and retrieved her registered parcel. Lola knew there were actually two Syndicate couriers; one of them would be a decoy. Neither courier knew who had the FLC package and who was the decoy. She decided if she was going to die, she wanted to know why, so she opened the package. What she didn't know was the moment the package was opened, a signal was sent back to a controller at The Syndicate who dispatched two contract hit men. The Syndicate rarely left their agents alive once they had served their purpose. In the past, Lola had been seen as important enough to be spared being removed, but this was different. She had disobeyed orders and opened the package. The Syndicate controller knew Lola was the decoy, so she would have to be eliminated.

Slim and Auntie had seen Lola coming from the post office with a parcel.

Wiggy said, 'Look, I think we have all had enough of this bullshit. Why don't we just go and kill her, get the bloody package and all go home?'

Slowpoke said she thought that would be very sensible. She and Auntie had been pooing their pants ever since they had got on the Orient Express. Brewster said he would be the one to do it as he was the one who befriended her on the train.

On his way to Lola's, he noticed up ahead the two Islamic men from the ferry, so he dropped back out of sight and followed. They were obviously going where he was going. He watched them ask the lady at the desk what room Lola was in and saw her pointing up at number 6. When Brewster got there and looked in through the window, he saw the two Iranians standing over Lola with their Glock pistols and an opened package on the table.

He heard them yelling, 'Where are they, you infidel? We will cut your breasts off and feed them to you, you brazen hussy.'

Brewster was deciding what to do when he saw Lola reach up to her neck, and quick as a flash, an ice pick was now buried in the small pimple-faced one's neck who was only knee high to a grasshopper, his life's blood pooling on the floor; he would be dead in thirty seconds. The large Iranian who looked like he could beat the shit out of a gorilla realised he couldn't kill Lola until he knew where the FLC package was, so he smacked her across the head, and she fell to the floor unconscious.

Brewster came through the door so quickly he caught the giant off guard. He shot the Glock out of his hand and managed to get another round into his side before he came at him. He picked up Brewster like a rag doll and threw him against the fridge. Brewster crawled up and kicked him in the kneecap. It dropped him in pain long enough to belt him across the head with a bread board. He shook his head, grabbed Brewster and launched him through the thin plywood wall into the next room.

The room was some sort of a printing room and there was a large paper guillotine with a steel blade that dropped down in a slide to cut paper and plastic. Brewster limped over and removed the pins that held the blade in its cradle and removed it. He limped back through the hole in the wall and saw the giant leaning over Lola. He raised the big steel cutting blade and buried it in the top of the giant's head. The giant turned around and shook his head but the blade was in so deep it never moved. The giant smiled at Brewster, and Brewster thought, *Well, I might as well have a go, I could now end up as pigeon shit.* The giant looked once more at Brewster and fell on his face, dead.

Lola looked up at Brewster.

'Jesus, how did you get here? What have you got to do with all this?' she said. 'But I'm glad you are, whatever it is. If you didn't keep reminding me of my father, I would have repaid you in kind. How old are you, Brewster?'

'You're looking at eighty-year-old man meat.'

'Jesus, are you mad? They should have retired you as an agent twenty years ago!'

'Oh, I'm not here by myself, There is another seven of us all about the same age. We're not actually agents.'

He told her how it all started and all the events that had occurred up until now.

'The sad part now is that I have to kill you, and that will be a sheer waste of a beautiful woman.'

Lola said, 'Well, before you do, there are some things you need to know. My real name is Lorraine, and I am a sleeping double agent for the Australian Security Intelligence Organisation (that's ASIO to you) and The Syndicate. I live with my husband and fourteen-year-old daughter at a place called Hidden Valley in country Victoria. Sleeping double agents never pass on valuable information of national security. We are more of a "listen and look" agent. We are activated for jobs like this, a courier of documentation or articles. We are never told what is in the package. The Syndicate ask me to deliver something, and I inform the CIA or vice versa. They may use that information if they think it's of value and I get paid twice. Being a double agent is bloody dangerous, but the money is good. My husband thinks I work as a courier for a diamond company delivering priceless diamonds to cashed-up customers. There were two couriers on this mission; one was a decoy. If you look at the package on the table, you will see I was the decoy, and the other Syndicate courier will have the real package, whatever and whoever that is. No one ever knows who a courier is, but they usually only use sleeper agent. It really hasn't made much difference. Russia will still treat me as the probable real package courier and will send more agents, along with contract killers for me from The Syndicate. You will need to talk to ASIO and MI6 for further instructions. I have broken the rules and opened the package, so my days as a double agent with The Syndicate are numbered and I wouldn't be surprised if those killers are on their way here as we speak.'

Brewster agreed to wait till he had spoken to those 'who must be obeyed'. Brewster made the call to MI6, who would inform ASIO, and they would get what intel they could from their undercover agents in The Syndicate. It would be at least another day before they would hear anything, and Brewster wasn't fit to travel with bruised ribs and kidneys, and he was still limping and in pain after the encounter with the giant.

The Spiders had a meeting, and it was decided to bring Lola into the fold for her own protection and their peace of mind on where she was. They all went out to Ristorante Villa '600, an Italian seafood restaurant on Torcello when you pay in lire. It seemed very expensive, but when they did the sums back to dollars, it was quite reasonable. While they were there, Lola was formally introduced to the Spiders of

Spy. Lola explained to the group what she had already told Brewster earlier on, and everyone seemed to warm to Lola, except Auntie who could see Lola was having just as much fun playing up to Brewster as he was with her. Auntie made sure Brewster wasn't sitting next to Lola by pushing him round between Slim and Wiggy. She thought he was over-enjoying himself where Lola was concerned. (To be truthful, she really wasn't that worried, because at his age, the only thing he could get hard would be his arteries.)

The word came back from MI6 and ASIO that Lola would stay as part of the team. Slim and Slowpoke were to go with her for extra support and the rest of the Spiders of Spy would go to London. Wiggy didn't think splitting up the Spiders was a good idea, and he told them. They agreed under some sufferance and sent them all back to London, 'but not on a bloody cruise,' they said.

The Kremlin was really pissed off that two of their agents from the KGB had gone offline. That usually meant they were dead, so they dispatched two more with the instructions that if they failed, they would spend the rest of their life in the salt mines. The Iranians were also concerned their agents should have been on a plane now with the FLC package. They would also be dispatching more agents for what seemed like a simple mission to take delivery of a package. The Syndicate had their money. The Iranians would be coming to get what they believed to be rightfully theirs, and the Russians were coming to steal it. They were all coming for nothing, but they didn't know that. The Spiders knew just telling them that they didn't have the FLC package wouldn't be good enough, and they would be really pissed off and kill them anyway.

The Spiders and Lola took the British Airways two-hour,

twenty-minute flight to London's Heathrow Airport where they had a big issue with the permits and their guns until airport security spoke to MI6, and then they were customs and security cleared. They were all booked in at the Park Plaza Westminster Bridge Hotel, a middle-of-the-road one as far as costs go. That night, the Spiders and Lola went to the Mei Ume Restaurant that served Chinese and Japanese food.

While they were there, Wiggy said, 'Jesus, these people have an unlimited supply of agents to keep throwing at us. They're all expendable to them so they're bound to keep coming after us. You do realise what's happening here, don't you? MI6 are using us as bloody bait to draw the baddies away while they go after the real courier and the FLC package, which I'm betting is a long way from where we are. It won't take the Russians and Iranians long to find out where we are. They think we still have the package; they will have no idea, Lola, that you were only a decoy courier. The Syndicate are smart. They wouldn't have dispatched the real courier until sufficient time had elapsed for you to suck the Russians and Iranian in to going after you, leaving the real courier free to deliver. So, I don't think we have to worry for too long about the Iranians. Now that the real courier is out and running, The Syndicate would have to advise the Iranians where the delivery will be made, and that will get them off our back. Of course, the Russians will know nothing about all this, and they will be coming hard and fast at us. As far as they're concerned, they think Lola still has the package. So we're in for more of this cloak-and-dagger shit.'

'We need to sit down and come up with our own defensive and retaliation plan before the bastards get here,' Slim said, 'Working on the theory that there's safety in numbers, we now only go places all together or in two groups of three. We can change who's in those groups whenever we want to. From now on, wear clothes with the zippered access to your gun at all times. Wiggy has volunteered to be "tail-end Charlie" wherever we go so we don't get hit from behind, and that will account for the seven of us. We also need an all-night security picket roster so that we don't get caught sleeping. We should also have a telltale hair or marker across the door for whenever we are out. We don't want any surprises when we come back. So, everyone, make sure you telltale your door when you leave. I know this all just sounds like simple things to do, but more often than not, simple is usually best. As Francis Drake said, *Parvis magna*; that's Latin for "great things from small things come".'

Brewster said, 'We can still treat this as a holiday, compliments of the government – sightseeing and going to shows ... Hopefully, MI6 and ASIO will now grab the package, and we can all go home, God and our expertise willing.'

They decided to get tickets to *Hello Dolly* that was showing at the London Palladium in Argyll Street. The tickets, a wine and a fine meal somewhere after the show were about 360 pounds each, they reckoned. They gave the problem of hiding it, together with other legitimate expenses like wine and beer and late-night card game snacks and the occasional pizza, to Tuppence to send to the government to reimburse. Considering what they were going through, the Finance Department wouldn't want to knock it back. They were never given any expense limit, but no one expected them to be in the field this long.

Chapter 7

Nadia, the real courier, was given her instructions from The Syndicate about the package and they informed her that the four smaller parts of the package were concealed in four false pearls in her necklace. She was only to give the necklace to the authorised person picking up the larger package with the correct passwords. When she said, 'Is there any rain about?', the correct response would be, 'It's supposed to rain tomorrow, and what a lovely necklace!' She could then give them the package and the pearl necklace. Once the Iranians were told this location and the correct password, she would hand over the package.

She was to keep moving until she received the location of the delivery point from The Syndicate. There were several places she would travel through for security, overnight at each place. The Syndicate orders came from somewhere in England, so it was presumed that's where the package would be leaving from. Nadia would be going to Germany by train, and to keep the travel as difficult to follow and as closed to public scrutiny as possible, Nadia would hop on a two-hour Eurostar service from London to Brussels, change to a high-speed Deutsche Bahn ICE service that took one hour and fifty minutes to Cologne and from there, on another slick ICE train where she could go to Munich, Frankfurt or Berlin. That was her mode of travel for her first leg.

While Nadia was getting on the train to Brussels, Victor and Boris were getting off Emirates Flight 304 at Heathrow Airport from Moscow and were staying at the Park Plaza County Hall, not far from where the Spiders were staying. They were the new agents sent from Russia. They knew exactly where the Spiders were as they were tracking them by their credit card activity. The Spiders of Spy, not being real agents, hadn't realised this was how they kept getting followed and found. So, they ditched their phones for burner phones that couldn't be traced.

The Syndicate were also aware that Agent Lola had gone offline. She could be dead but this was of no concern, as she was only the decoy. Even if she wasn't dead, she would still be playing her role leading the enemy agents away while the real package was being delivered. Victor and Boris decided that whenever the Spiders went anywhere, one of them would follow and the other would search their rooms.

The Spiders decided to go to The Cinnamon Club for their evening meal. They left separately in their planned two lots of threes, with Wiggy following discreetly behind. Wiggy saw a man come out of the shadows and follow along behind them. Wiggy made a phone call to Slim to let them know they were being followed.

'Don't look back. I'm on to him. If he tries anything, I can shoot him from where I am, no worries.'

They went into the restaurant and whoever he was turned away and disappeared. Slim checked for emergency exits and alternate ways to get out if they had to; he checked the rest room and asked the girls to do the same. They didn't see the mystery man again that night but when they got back, all the door telltales were broken. Someone had been in all the rooms. Whoever it was had been very professional; you couldn't tell that anything had been disturbed.

Slim said, 'We should do the same tomorrow night as we did tonight. I will purchase some "presents" for our new friends if they come into the restaurant tomorrow night.'

The next night, when they headed off to the restaurant, two men followed them. The Spiders were casually ambling along with Slim carrying a small bag. The men followed them into the restaurant and sat at a table.

Boris said to Victor, 'I will wait till one of them goes to the toilet by himself and I'll take him out.'

Halfway through the meal, Wiggy and Slim went to the toilets, carrying a bag. In the bag was two small bottles full of nitroglycerine, a small book of matches (the type you would get at a night club), a roll of sticky tape, a reel of cotton and half a cigarette and a handwritten sign that said, 'Out of order'. There were two cubicles. They tied the cotton around the necks of the bottles of nitroglycerine and hung them from the ceiling, taped a book of matches to the cotton, with the cotton in among the matches, and poked the half-cigarette into the match book and lit the cigarette. They locked the door, crawled out under the door space, stuck the out of order sign on the door and returned to their table.

Slim got up and went to the toilet with Boris following. Slim got to the door first and held it open for Boris. As Boris went in, Slim slid the outside bolt across the door and hurried back to the table. The Russian was now locked in. The cigarette burnt down to the matches which ignited and burnt through the cotton. The cotton broke, the nitroglycerine bottles fell to the floor and broke, and the nitroglycerine exploded. Say goodbye to Boris and the toilets. In the restaurant, everybody panicked and ran outside. The Spiders watched the other bloke hurriedly disappearing into the darkness.

Victor realised they were dealing with old but very clever people who would need to be treated with caution. He also realised he would need reinforcements, or he would be dead or going to the salt mines, and he wasn't going there because of a bunch of bloody pensioners. So, he had asked the Kremlin for more support. The Spiders didn't know if these new two were Russians or the Iranians, but Slowpoke said they didn't look like camel drivers to her; she thought they were more like Russians.

Lola said, 'Look they have my photo, so they know who I am, so I think I will deal with this other bloke that was at the restaurant. but I need to do this by myself. Hopefully, he will follow me to the Tube tomorrow and we will be rid of him.'

Wiggy said he would follow along behind them and be her eyes.

The next morning, Wiggy followed Lola to Waterloo station. He moved down the platform so that when they got on the train, he was in a different carriage and not seen. It was morning peak hour, and the train was packed with passengers.

Lola moved up right next to Victor and said, 'I know who you are, but I don't have the package. I was just the decoy, so I'm asking you stop the senseless killing for nothing.'

He said, 'Do you think I am stupid?'

Lola said, 'No I don't, but I think you're dead. Little boys should do as they're told.'

She rammed the ice pick up his nose into his brain and quickly disappeared among the morning crowded passengers. When Lola and Wiggy got back, she told them they could rest easy for a while.She had killed him with a nose job.

The girls asked, 'How you do that?'

Wiggy said, 'Don't ask. You won't like it.'

*　*　*

The Supreme Leader of the Islamic Republic, Ali Khamenei, called a meeting with the members of the Guardian Council.

'Someone owes us $250 million or the FLC package which we have paid for, so why is it so hard to collect what's rightfully ours.?'

'Sir, there are other countries that want these chips and are prepared to go to any lengths to steal them. We have lost several agents already. The woman they call Lola has the package and the agents we sent to meet her in Istanbul have gone offline, and since we have had no contact from them, they are presumed dead. The woman called Lola is finding it difficult protecting the package from other countries and finding a safe place for delivery to us.'

'Right, let's have no more of this bullshit. This time, send two male agents and one female, dispose of the opposition and bring home the package. We have photos of Lola and we're tracking her via a credit card. Just make sure we send Janat, Haseeb and Usman. They are to give us a Sit Rep every twenty-four hours. Get them on their way ASAP!'

*　*　*

After the long arduous journey and changing of trains, Nadia was tired and stressed out from watching for boogeymen who weren't there. Several times she'd had her gun out of her handbag concealed in her lap. She was staying at the Hotel Oderberger, two kilometres from what is left of the Berlin Wall. She would only be there for one night.

The Russians had also realised that their agents were also out of the game. The Russian president, who supervised the division of the KGB into several major services responsible for internal security and foreign intelligence, called a meeting with the chairman of the KGB and his six deputies.

'I won't keep accepting these failures. The next failure will have serious consequences we are being made to look like fools. Get Makail and Igor over there, and get that package!'

*　*　*

The Spiders decided to rent a people mover, a seven-seater Vauxhall Zafira Tourer. They didn't want to get caught somewhere on foot with no fast quick getaway, and they didn't want to be exposed on public transport, having to keep watch on all angles at once. And now they had a choice: where they would normally have travelled by public transport, they would drive, and they would walk short distances using their safe system of two by three, with Wiggy as "tail end Charlie". They didn't know their way around London, but if the shit hit the fan, they would just drive like buggery and make it up as they went along.

They decided they needed some extra equipment and now that they had the car, they could use it to store things and take it wherever they went, so they asked trick and treat man

Slim to make a list and then they would go shopping.

Slim said, 'I've only put these items on the list in case we are really boxed in somewhere. We will probably never need them. You know what they say – hope for the best, prepare for the worst. It simply means, be a person of action and prepare yourself for when the hard times hit. Hopefully, we won't shoot some poor innocent bastard in the crowd.'

The Spiders went shopping for the items on Slim's list: double braided nylon, a heavy-duty magnet with fastening ring, one extra 9 mm magazine each, 350 nine-mm rounds (fifty each), a small Hot Devil, handheld blowtorch, high-powered binoculars, seven cigarette lighters and a small plastic lightweight heavy-duty hook with fastening ring. They took a cigarette lighter each and Slim showed everyone how to use the blowtorch, and then they neatly put the rest of the items in the back of the Vauxhall. They had also moved from the Park Plaza after blowing up the toilet at the restaurant and were now staying at The Pilgrm in Westminster, three kilometres from the city centre.

Brewster, who hadn't said much the last couple of days, said, 'I think we should work out how big our threat actually might be.'

'Right,' said Wiggy, 'there will be two agents from The Syndicate coming for Lola, at least two from Russia to try for the package and at least two from Iran to make sure they get what they consider theirs. So that is six of them, which could drop back to four when The Syndicate tell the Iranians where the real courier is.'

'Jesus,' Tuppence said, 'we've disposed of six of them already. The bastards will just keep coming till the FLC package disappears.'

The three Iranians had now arrived and were staying not far away at the Royal Eagle Hotel in Paddington. They knew where Lola was staying by her credit card activity, and as they didn't know the Spiders even existed, they assumed Lola was on her own with no support. Hugo and Milo, the two contract killers who had come for Lola from The Syndicate, had also just arrived in London and were staying at the same hotel as the Iranians. Whether that would prove to be good or bad, time would tell.

The Spiders put everyone's choices for the evening meal in a hat and drew them out.

'Looks like we're having pizza,' said Slowpoke and Auntie.

They looked up where to go, and everyone seemed happy with Alley Cats Pizza, about three kilometres away so they would drive. Alley Cats Pizza was unique with its gingham tablecloths, and there were queues of expectant diners waiting for one of these tables. They started with scrumptious, rich, basil infused meatballs with tomato sauce and then a perfect thin crusted pepperoni pizza. They would definitely be eating there again.

Ever since they had been in London, they had become used to keeping the silencers on their guns. If they had to use them, they wouldn't draw unnecessary attention to themselves.

On the way back to the hotel, Auntie said, 'I could be wrong, but I think there's a green Volvo following us two cars back.'

Everyone except Wiggy, who was driving, looked back.

Wiggy said, 'I'll drive around the block, and let's see what the Volvo does.'

They drove around several side streets to get back to where they had started. When they looked back, the Volvo was still there.

Slim said, 'Well, looks like the first of the partygoers have arrived. I wonder which ones they are.'

Wiggy said, 'Right, let's see if this bastard can drive, and then I'll try and draw him alongside. Then, windows down and give them their party presents.'

They flew down Marylebone Road at 100 mph. They took the left fork on to Sussex Gardens, left into Edgware Road and right into Connaught Street. Now they had no idea where they were. Mind you, they knew those in the Volvo wouldn't know either. They were now in some heavy traffic, with the Volvo stuck in the left lane. The Spiders were in the right lane, which was moving faster than the partygoers.

Wiggy said, 'Windows down and deliver their presents.'

Slim and Brewster emptied their magazines into the windows of the car. Wiggy pulled forward to give clear shots at the windscreen. Auntie and Slowpoke fired their guns next to both Slim's ears, nearly deafening him, as they had forgotten to screw on their silencers. They shot about twelve holes in the windscreen which now had a red stain on what was left of the glass. The partygoers had nowhere to go; they were sitting ducks wedged in the left lane of traffic. The Spiders looked back in time to see the Volvo leave their side of the road and smash into the traffic in the outside lane.

'Time to get out of Dodge,' Wiggy said.

Thankfully they were in the fast outside lane. and they spun off down the next side street, arguing about which was the best way back and hoping no one took their number plate.

They watched the BBC Home News that night. The authorities thought it was a rival drug cartel, as the two passengers who had been shot dead had British passports with false addresses and false names. The police were not looking for anyone else at this time. They had to explain what the the man on the TV was saying for Slim; he was still deaf, thanks to Auntie and Slowpoke firing next to his ears.

Slim said to Lola, 'Do you Know where The Syndicate operates from?'

'The head of the snake is somewhere in England, but no one knows where.'

'Well, if I had to make a choice, I would bet those two were from The Syndicate. Mind you, I've been wrong before – just ask Slowpoke – but there's a fair chance I'm right this time. They will send someone else, of course, when those two don't check in. But it knocks another two party gatecrashers off our list for a while anyway.'

'What I want to know,' said Brewster, 'is how they keep knowing exactly where we are.'

Tuppence said, 'Lola, are you using your credit card?'

'Yes.'

'Well, there's your answer. They are all tracking us by Lola's bloody credit card activity. The Syndicate gave you the name "Lola". That's how they know your name, and so does everyone else. Do you have another credit card?'

'Yes, but I don't want to use it; otherwise, they will know where I live in real life, and that would endanger my family.'

Tuppence said, 'You go to the bank two days after we book in and use your normal credit card to draw cash. Book in using cash but we can keep using our cards. That way, you won't be using your card the same day the Spiders book in, so there will be no connection to us. You can stay in my room for that one night. They don't know our names, which is why everybody thinks you're here by yourself with no support, and also why we're getting the drop on them. They're not expecting anyone else to be in play, but that won't last either. So, now we know how they are doing it, we will all need new accommodation. They will certainly know where we are staying at the moment.'

Slowpoke said, 'We need to start thinking about our safety when choosing accommodation, somewhere where we don't have to keep going out at night for meals, which is the biggest risk. We can eat out for lunch if we want but be home safe at night, the most vulnerable time for us. And by the way, Lola, don't use your phone anymore. Give it to me, and I'll take the chip out of it. Otherwise, even if it's turned off, they can track it.'

They used Brewster's phone to find a place to stay. They decided on somewhere outside London, forty-five minutes away out of harm's way at Danesfield House near Henley-on-Thames. It had its own dining room for breakfas and the evening meal, so it was perfect. Renting the car was a good idea.

Wiggy said, 'And if MI6 along with ASIO want us to stay and risk our lives, they can bloody well pay for a bit of comfort. Christ, we could all be dead tomorrow!'

*   *   *

The Russians and Iranians had been separately watching for Lola for two days and had not seen her, so they separately enquired at the desk and were told she had booked out with her friends. Now they knew she was no longer by herself. But their efforts to track her again had all failed, so they would have to think now what to do next.

The Iranians already knew the Spiders had a car, as Lola's credit card had been used – another mistake they had made, sharing expenses on credit cards. The Russians now paid a visit to the car rental company and said they had some friends whose phones weren't working, and they needed to find them.

They said, 'No worries. All of our cars have trackers installed.'

'Where is the car now?'

'It's at Danesfield House near Henley-on-Thames.

*   *   *

The Spiders and Lola went down for breakfast and ordered an English Breakfast. When the food came out, there were back bacon, sausages, poached eggs, fried tomatoes, baked beans, black pudding, toast and fried bread, a hearty breakfast to start the day.

Auntie said, 'We need to somehow find out who has arrived here in London in the last couple of days. How do we do that?'

'The problem is we don't have any names,' said Brewster. 'Bugger it, ask MI6 to check customs for anyone coming in from Russia or Iran in the last week, and we can sort it out from there.'

MI6 left a message on Wiggy's phone. Yes, two days ago, two Russian males arrived from Saint Petersburg and two male and one female from Isfahan in Iran.

Brewster said, 'So the gangs all here then. I see they have heard about my good looks and charm and sent a female to get a look at a good Aussie bloke.'

'The only looking she will be doing is to see which part of

your swollen head to shoot at,' Auntie said.

They decided to familiarise themselves with the outside grounds. Danesfield House had an impressive tree-lined drive with hornbeam trees under the clock tower, box hedges filled with a variety of English and French lavender and over twenty-six hectares of woodland and gardens surrounding the house, a lot of which was covered by purple wisteria.

All very nice, but they were more interested in the twenty-six hectares of woodland and where it went to if you went through it. Slim and Brewster walked through and on the other side was a small car park and children's playground. They walked back to tell the others.

Lola asked them, 'Did you have a bit of a go on the swings and slide while you were there?'

Slim said, 'Very funny, Lola.'

Tomorrow they would see how to get to the playground by car. That way, if they needed to, they could park the car and walk back to the hotel through the woodland.

While they were on the edge of the woodland, they saw a yellow Volkswagen drive into the hotel car park, and two men and a woman get out and enter the building. They quickly checked the car – it was from the same rental company where they had hired the Vauxhall.

'Jesus,' Wiggy said, 'you don't suppose––?'

'Yes, we do,' said Slim.

'How could they have found us so quickly?'

'Buggered if I know,' Brewster said.

'Well, said Tuppence, 'I'll bet we used Lola's bloody credit card again.'

'Yes, we did,' said Lola, 'but that wouldn't tell them where we are.'

Slim said, 'I'll bet you all the rental cars, including ours, have trackers fitted and they asked them where our car was parked. And as bad luck happened, it was parked here and not in London somewhere. Bloody rotten luck. Jesus, we will have to move again and find another car one that doesn't have a tracker.'

They found a rental Toyota people mover and explained that it was important that there was no tracking device on the car because it affected Slim's pacemaker. They were guaranteed there was no tracking device on the car, and Slim paid with his credit card. Now they would look for new accommodation, and this time, they should be okay.

They all agreed it was still a good idea to find a place outside London where they didn't have to go out at night. After several discussions about safety and security, they decided on Rothay Manor Hotel in Ambleside in the Lakes District. All rooms had their own balconies overlooking the hotel car park where they could set up a twenty-four-hour watching picket. Slowpoke said she would pay for Lola's room on her credit card and Lola could pay her when she got cash.

* * *

The Syndicate had contracted Hugo from Glasgow and Milo from Canada, both contract killers, to dispose of Lola. They were sent photos of her and were told of her last known place, thanks to her recent credit card activity. They went to Danesfield House, but she was no longer there.

* * *

Nadia was told the package could be handed over in transit or in situ, so she was always on edge when she was travelling. Every time someone came near her, she imagined they were going to be the ones she was waiting for.

She would be catching the Nightjet train leaving Berlin at 6.30 pm, arriving in Vienna at 7.00 am the next day. She had a sleeping berth so she could lock herself in the cabin. There was no dining car but she could get breakfast delivered to her cabin. She would be staying at the Leonardo Hotel Vienna Hauptbahnhof, directly opposite the main railway station. She was trying to be security conscious, but at the same time, she had to make herself available for the package transfer, and that was proving difficult to achieve at the same time.

* * *

Lola said she needed to go to the bank and draw some money, seeing she couldn't use her credit cards, so they chose the Royal Bank of Scotland at 1 Princes Street, London. They went together in the car, following the safety in numbers theory, but their luck was about to change. Lola went into the bank. Janat and Haseeb, the Iranian agents, were in the bank changing their rials into pounds, and Usman was waiting outside in the car. When the Spiders got back from driving around the block, Lola was nowhere to be seen. Even worse, the Russians had been following the Iranians everywhere to get ahead on where Lola was. Now they knew where everyone was.

Brewster's phone rang. It was Janat.

'We will trade Lola for the package, or she is dead. It's up to you. We will be in touch.'

'Jesus, this is not good! We need to ring MI6,' said Auntie.

They made the call and were told to follow the Iranian's instructions. They were very close to securing the package from Vienna, but things needed to stay cool at this end for that to happen. Tell Slowpoke this would be a good time to enlighten everyone of her expertise, and good luck.'

'So, what's all this expertise about?' asked Slim.

'A long time ago, before we were married,' she said, smiling at Slim, 'I was trained as an MI6 and ASIO agent and taught to use all weapons proficiently in unarmed combat and counterintelligence and I was sworn to secrecy. When we were married, I retired but still couldn't tell anyone, which is why I had to play-act with the gun. As you just heard, I can speak to you about it now.'

'Jesus, 'Slim said, 'I'm glad I didn't give you too much cheek. I could have been beaten up badly. So much for the shooting of holes in the handbag.'

It didn't take long for the Iranian's phone call: 'Tomorrow, 10 am. Bring the package to the old London Pumping Station. If we see anyone else, we kill the woman.'

The Pumping Shed was a huge building with labyrinthine alleyways, high vaulted ceilings, mezzanines and raised iron gangways, and a push beam girder trolley for block and tackle, but it was now just a derelict shadow of its former self.

Wiggy would carry the coil of double braided rope and the magnet, Brewster would have the small plastic hook, everyone would have their extra magazines and extra rounds and Slim would carry the small Hot Devil blowtorch. Wiggy thought they couldn't have been better prepared than they were. It was the old 'seven Ps': prior preparation and planning prevents piss poor performance.

They parked on the other side of the road and used the binoculars to scan the building. There were two cars parked outside, but they wouldn't be going in the front. It looked like they could drive round the block and come in undetected from the rear, so that's what they did.

When they got inside, a voice from somewhere above said, 'Come up, but only one of you.'

They all looked at each other until Slowpoke said, 'I'll go.'

Knowing what they knew now about her, they all shrugged and said okay. Slowpoke went up the steel stairs to the catwalk. Janat came out of a small room at the other end, pushing Lola out in front of her.

'Wow, how old are you people?'

'Just the right age to put your lights,' Slowpoke said.

'Where's the package?

'We don't have it. Lola was only a decoy.'

Lola said, 'I have been trying to tell them that. Your country should have been told where the real package is by now.'

Both Janat and Slowpoke had their guns trained on each other, when suddenly gunfire erupted from down where the Spiders were waiting.

'That will be the Russians,' Slowpoke said. 'They also think we have the package. We can work together to get rid of the Russians, who are both our enemies, and work towards some peace in a turbulent world.'

'Can you be trusted?' Janat said.

'As one agent to another, yes, I can.'

The Iranians went downstairs to see the Spiders, so they wouldn't be shot as the enemy.

'Wow,' Janat said, 'you're all old age people! You'll all be killed.'

'Not likely,' said Slowpoke, and shot a light globe out from fifty metres away.

'Bloody show-off,' Slim said.

The Russians had split up.

'Seven verses two – this won't take long,' said Brewster.

But there were so many nooks and crannies and blind spots to be shot from, it wasn't that simple. Everyone had split up, so now people were sneaking around a half-lit two-storey factory, and someone was going to get shot who shouldn't.

Auntie was crouching behind the two boilers waiting for someone to shoot. Brewster had found a locked door and was smashing it down with a forklift. Upstairs there was gunfire and the sound of bullets ricocheting off metal walls.

Wiggy was taking gunfire from both ends of the catwalk, Igor at one end and Mikail at the other, with nowhere to go while trying to return the gunfire. He took the double braided thin rope from round his shoulder, tied the heavy-duty magnetic disk on and threw it across the gap to the catwalk on the other side. A lucky first throw saw the disc fastened to the metal walkway. Wiggy jumped over the rail and swung down to the ground floor. Igor was leaning over the handrail to see where Wiggy had gone when Slowpoke came up behind him, and over he went. Wiggy flipped the rope cable and pressed the button on the small demagnify hand control, and the heavy magnetic disc came down on Igor's head.

There was a large steel door that led to a separate part of the factory. Janat called out, 'He has gone through here.' The seven of them were standing at a heavy steel door that had been locked from the other side. They could have all gone out and round the back to get in but by the time they got out of the factory and round to the other side, the Russian would be long gone.

Slim said, 'Get out of the way. Let the dog see the rabbit.'

He fired up his Hot Devil blowtorch and cut a hole in the steel casing so they could get to the lock, and they all went through.

This part of the factory was a maze of narrow metal stairs and steel catwalks with handrails, large cast iron wheels that operated the chain lifting and pulley system, two more large boilers and a conveyor belt that delivered large stones to a crushing machine. The rocks fell into a large steel container with cutting blades and crushing rollers. This part of the factory was darker than the front part. Lola tried the main power box, and to her surprise, it was still live. She turned on the lights, and some of the machines sprung into life. They had just been left on and turned off via the power box. The conveyor belt and crusher were also operating.

Brewster saw something move behind the two boilers and carefully moved over. Mikail was crouching down, looking the other way. Brewster cracked him across the head and knocked him out. Janat, Haseeb and Usman picked him up like a rag doll and threw him onto the conveyor belt. They watched him travel along the conveyor belt and fall into the crushing tub. Lumps of crushed flesh, skin and bone and blood spewed out the other side.

Janat said, 'We will now find out where the real courier is and get what is rightfully ours.'

The Spiders made no comment, but they knew that wasn't true.

The Iranians went off, and the Spiders were waiting for Auntie who had gone off looking for a toilet. Auntie came back but she wasn't alone. Hugo and Milo from The Syndicate had followed the Iranians to the Pumping Station and had been waiting outside to see who had survived. Now they were inside. Auntie had been grabbed by Milo and now she had a bomb strapped on. Hugo had the control to start the timer with Milo smiling standing next to him.

'We want the package, or we start the timer,' Milo said.

'We haven't got the package and never did have. Lola was only the decoy, so we can't help you,' Slim said.

'Don't give us that bullshit,' they said. 'Well, it looks like we will have to activate the bomb,' said Milo.

Hugo flicked the switch, and the timer started the countdown from three minutes as they both hightailed it out of the pump shed.

Auntie said, 'I often wondered how I might die. I had hoped I would just die in bed one night, not blown to bits pretending to be a super sleuth.'

'Shut up, Auntie,' they said. 'We are thinking.'

Slowpoke said, 'I can't remember if I cut the red off or the green first. It's been a long time but we were taught a catchphrase, but I can't remember if R is for right so cut the red, or is R for wrong, so cut the gree n...'

The bomb counter was now down to thirty seconds.

Tuppence said, 'Well, "right" starts with an R so does the word "red", but "wrong" starts with a W.'

They cut the red wire, and the bomb counter stopped. They pulled the bomb off Auntie, and she gave Slowpoke and Tuppence a kiss.

'Jesus, if I was still an agent, I would get that tattooed on my arm somewhere,' Slowpoke said.

The Iranians told their colleagues they had been chasing

nothing all this time and were waiting for further instructions. The Russians would be sending more agents when they got the intel of the package location, depending on how good their intel was. The only ones the Spiders had concerns about now were Hugo and Milo who wanted Lola dead as per The Syndicate's orders.

The CIA and a MI6 were going to send them all home but because everyone knew that London was only a decoy, there would now be a switch of agents to Vienna. The chances of Lola being known on the agents' circuits were good, so she was being removed as a player and sent back to Australia. Hugo and Milo, The Syndicate killers, had been tailing the Spiders so they knew Lola wasn't going with them.

The Spiders were being sent to Vienna to even up the numbers of other agents that would now be sent there.

'They still don't realise how old we are,' said Wiggy.

'Yes, they do,' said Slim, 'They just don't give a shit. Where were the agents from the so-called mighty ASIO and MI6? We have not seen any of them the whole time. They have been using the brains of retired seventy- and eighty-year-olds from whom they will claim the credit or excuses, depending on what the final outcome is. How easy would it be to blame retired geriatrics and tell the authorities you don't know how they got involved, or play their part down if the end results were good. You see, they can't bloody lose; they will always have an out. That's always been the government's way. It doesn't matter who gets in the shit as long as their arse is covered.'

So, the Spiders were going to Vienna. They were going by Flixbus from London via Belgium and Czechoslovakia to Vienna, staying at the Steigenberger Hotel Herrenhof.

They were sitting in the Hard Rock Café at Piccadilly

Circus having lunch, when Wiggy said, 'Let me run something past you; tell me what you think. Has anyone ever seen this bloody so-called FLC package? No. Even those who are after it have never seen it. The closest anyone has got is to see an empty box that Lola had. And why haven't they just handed it over to the Iranians who say they have paid for it? Why would you travel all around the globe, giving the other countries more chances to steal it, spending huge amounts of money for travel and accommodation and meals? It could easily have been handed over ten times already that we know of. I wouldn't mind betting the other package doesn't exist either, and that the courier in Vienna has an empty box as well.'

'Well,' Tuppence said, 'what you're saying is correct. Can't argue with that. So given you're right, why are they, whoever they are, doing this?'

Slim said, 'That's the million dollar question. It's obviously a smoke-and-mirrors screen for something else that's going on that we're not privy to. MI6, ASIO or someone else is doing this, and our mob are too dumb to see what's going on. We're going to Vienna tomorrow. We will try and figure all this out when we get there.'

Chapter 8

t was nearly a twenty-four-hour journey from London to Vienna, so on arrival they slept for a few hours to make up for the restless night on the bus. It was doubtful that Milo and Hugo would follow them to Vienna as they knew that Lola was no longer with them, and that would be a blessing – two less to worry about. Their priority, as they saw it, was to uncover what the smokescreen was for. That's if they had read it right; maybe they were wrong. But it was certainly worth investigating till it gave up some answers.

The next day, they rented a Renault Trafic nine-seater van. Now the trick was to find out where the courier was. They didn't know who they were or where they came from. And if their package was empty, they wouldn't know that either.

* * *

Ziggy Oliver had been the assistant manager of Paramount Financial Services in London when he had been sentenced for the embezzlement of $2.5 million. His ego and self-pity were bigger than his brains, and he considered the world owed him a living. It was all about payback from the system that wouldn't allow him to be part of his corrupt world and reap the benefits of his ill-gotten gains. He had ten years in the Iron Gate Detention Centre and the money he had embezzled to come up with his plan.

His cellmate was a man called Silas who had once worked at the Government Serum Laboratories. He gave Ziggy the name of a friend who was less than honest who had access to whatever you needed. After paying out a considerable amount of money, Ziggy had obtained ten ampoules of the coronavirus germ. He had been released from prison now for three months and had put his plan into action.

He knew about the FLC package circulating out there somewhere, and that would fit in nicely with moving the ampoules. He put the FLC information on the dark web and the illegal cyber night watch web to make sure it was well known, and he had provided ASIO and MI6 with some of the details of his plan, enough information to get them interested. He had paid a large amount of money to Lola, a sleeping agent with ASIO and a double agent for The Syndicate, to be a false courier to start the ball rolling. If ASIO didn't use her (which would entice others into the game), there were others who had to be paid to keep it all moving along smoothly. The plan was devised to keep ASIO and MI6 busy worrying about the FLC chips, while he moved the ampoules along to their destination. Given they were responsible for uncovering organised crime and terrorist activity, he would let the plan develop and grow until he was ready to talk to them again about the ampoules.

The package that Nadia was carrying for Ziggy had five of the coronavirus ampoules, although she didn't know what was in the package. Ziggy had just released another courier in Australia with the other five coronavirus ampoules.

Brian, the military police dude, and the Colonel went to see Nitro and Sparkie on the pretence to see how Sparkie was getting along, but it was really to ask for their help. They knew that Sparkie had fully recovered and was back to her old ways. She was also the youngest of the Spiders, only sixty-eight.

After they had done the 'How are you? You're looking fantastic and younger every time we see you' bullshit, they said they had recently received information that another courier with the FLC was on their way to a place called Lakes Entrance on the east coast of Victoria and now they were concerned. There was supposed to be only the one set of FLC ever produced and that was in Europe somewhere, so something wasn't right.

Nitro said, 'What do you think, Marie? We could ask Max and Jane if we could stay at their place while all this is going on. If that's okay with them, we will do it. At least we will see this nightmare through to the end – that's if we're not all bloody dead!'

* * *

Lilly was a private contractor on the dark web who guaranteed the delivery of illegal packages and drugs, and she was paid a handsome sum by Ziggy to take the package to Lakes Entrance and wait for instructions. She would be flying in from Durango in Mexico and getting the package from airport locker number 612 with the code 8800 to open the box. The package, like the others, had a pass code number to open the parcel. No one else had been given the code numbers.

She had flown into Melbourne on Air Canada flight 400 at 9.30 pm. She stayed at the airport's Travelodge a hundred metres away, where she hired a black Jaguar F-Pace SUV from Budget Car Hire nearby. She was now staying at the Bellevue Motel at Lakes Entrance where she was to wait for further instructions. She had done a reconnaissance of Lakes Entrance and found there was virtually just one way in and one way out. That could be a problem. She made some enquiries with locals about another way out. They showed her two other ways that were much longer but that wouldn't leave her trapped in Lakes Entrance. Lakes Entrance has a population of approximately eight thousand which is boosted by another twenty-five thousand at Christmas time, so she hoped she would be gone by then. Anyway, if things started to look shaky, she would leave immediately and leave the package in a mailbox.

* * *

Wiggy and Tuppence had told Nitro and Marie they could stay at Fairview, no problems. The Spiders' biggest problem was how to find the courier in Vienna.

MI6 had contacted them with information that a man and a woman had just arrived in Vienna on a flight from Moscow. The passenger information supplied by Etihad was that the two most likely passengers were Zarina Petrov and Ivan Novikov who had prearranged bookings at the Hilton Vienna Waterfront.

'So, how does that help?' said Auntie.

'Well, they will have better intelligence than we do. So, we watch for them outside their hotel and when we think we see a man and woman who look Russian coming out, we go in and ask for them. If we're told they have just gone out, we'll know it's them, and if it's not them, we do it all again,' said Slim.

They were lucky the first time. It always amused Brewster how people from different countries just looked different – not that you could always tell what country.

After two days, the Russians, with the Spiders close behind, had tracked Nadia down. She had gone into a chemist's for a prescription. The Russians waited outside, the Spiders went in. When the chemist called out, 'Nadia Fox' and when she went to the counter for the prescription, they now knew her and her name. She was a plumpish woman with black curly hair, a small squinty nose and too much makeup. Like the Russians, they followed her to her hotel. Once again, the Russians waited outside and the Spiders went in.

'We're visiting Nadia Fox.'

'She's in room 312.'

Their plan was to somehow place one of those small luggage trackers on her somewhere, so they always knew where she would be – that was the difficult part. As they walked down the passageway on level 3, there was a large clothes rack on wheels, presumably with dry cleaning being delivered to the owners' rooms. The clothes all had dry cleaning tags with room numbers pinned on. Their luck was holding out; there was a coat with the tag 312 pinned on it, hanging among the other clothes. They quickly attached the small luggage tracker to the bottom seam of the coat and left.

Back outside the hotel, the Russians had gone.

* * *

Nadia was on the move again. This time she was told to go by the Nightjet train to Rome where she would be staying at the Hotel Santa Prassede. She was given a phone number to contact a Giorgio Russo in three days' time. With the right passwords, he would pick up the package at a place designated by him.

*   *   *

The Russians had gone back to check on Nadia, but she had booked out and hotel management said she hadn't left a forwarding address.

Zarina said, 'That's great! we have to wait now for more intel from Moscow.'

The Spiders were checking the tracker in Nadia's coat every few hours and it was on the move in the direction of Rome, so they took the train the next day and booked in at the Palazzo Ripetta. Zarina and Ivan hadn't been in the Spiders' location long enough to know who the Spiders were, so they wouldn't be following them to Rome.

Janat, Haseeb and Usman had gathered enough intel from their authorities to realise the real FLC package was in Vienna. But they had also learnt of the possibility of another package in Australia. They were to stay in Vienna with this one, and other agents would be sent for the package in Australia. When they got to Vienna, they, like the Russians, learnt Nadia had gone. The Russians and the Iranians now knew her name, so they would wait for any credit card or phone activity. Hopefully, that would be sooner than later; otherwise, she would be gone again when they got there.

ASIO and MI6 were now so concerned about the second package they had up scaled their support from England and New Zealand. They were concerned about the FLC getting into the wrong hands – they had always been worried about that – but something wasn't right. They had their own reasons to be worried, and it was nothing to do with what was going on in Europe.

Ziggy decided the time was right. He rang MI6 and ASIO and told them The Syndicate was about to hand over the FLC package to the Russians, but this was only a smokescreen. The package in Rome had five ampoules of coronavirus and so did the package in Lakes Entrance. He said he wanted $1 million in the next eight hours, or each hour over, one ampule would be released into the atmosphere in a crowded place in Lakes Entrance and Rome's Termini train station. The eight-hour timer would begin at midday the day after tomorrow.

*   *   *

Nadia rang the number she had been given and asked for Giorgio Russo. She said who she was. He said, 'MagicLand Amusement Park, midday, the day after tomorrow. Wear a red scarf,' and hung up.

The Spiders had tracked her down with the luggage tracker to the Hotel Santa Prassede. They followed her on foot to the Felice a Testaccio restaurant. In Rome, they eat the evening meal anywhere between 8 and 10 pm, and since it was 7 pm, they followed her in. What an amazing place with its retro checked floors and white tablecloths! They all ordered the signature dish, *cacio e pepe*, a tangle of spaghetti with melted cheese and black pepper freshly tossed at the table. Nadia was sitting at a table by herself, and since Brewster considered himself as God's gift to woman, they sent him over.

He said, 'Hello there. We noticed you were by yourself, and we would like you to join us for dinner.'

She said, 'That would be nice. I have been on my own the last couple of days. It would be nice to have someone to talk to for a change.'

She sat down with them. Brewster poured her a glass of wine with Auntie glaring at him and giving him a kick under the table. After they did the normal 'Hello. Where are you from? Are you on holidays? and so on, they learnt that she was delivering a package for a company called The Syndicate. She was not aware of the contents, but it must be important because she was being paid a lot of money. She didn't ask any questions as it wasn't her business what was in the box. She also had a pearl necklace that went with the package, and she had to give a special password. She said she thought it was a little strange that she had to travel to all these places.

'I don't understand if I'm delivering the package here tomorrow. Why wasn't I just sent straight here? But again, it's none of my business. I will deliver it in two days' time and fly home.'

The Russians and the Iranians were on the same flight to Rome, although they didn't know each other. Unfortunately for Nadia, she had used her credit card, so they now knew where Nadia was staying, and that was all they needed to know. The Russians were booked into the same hotel as Nadia and the Iranians at the Hotel Nazionale. They had been watching Nadia's every move, and so had the Spiders who were still trying to second-guess what was going on.

'Well, here's what we think so far,' said Slim. 'I reckon

whatever is in the box is not what everyone thinks is in there. Russia and Iran still think the FLC are in the package. I think they're in for a surprise. But whatever is in there, it's important enough to ferry it all over Europe. Nadia has no idea; she's just doing it for the money. We need to stay really close tomorrow when she makes the delivery.'

The next day, Nadia was picked up in the park's courtesy bus and driven to Valmontone where the fun park was, with its roller-coasters and a sky wheel. There were now eleven people interested in the package: three from Iran, two from Russia and the six Spiders.

Giorgio spotted Nadia and beckoned her to follow. He had two tickets for the sky wheel, and seeing that's where they were going, so did all the Spiders except Tuppence. When the cage with Giorgio and Nadia got to the top, he threw her out. Her body hit all the super-structure on the way down, so she was dead by the time she hit the ground. When Giorgio's cage reached ground level, Tuppence shot him dead.

Slim was in a cage with Wiggy, two cages down from Zarina and Ivan, and Slim somehow shot Ivan through his ear hole. When Zarina's cage was level with the ground, she jumped out but was hit by the cage coming down behind her. Wiggy made the comment, 'Well, she's dead on arrival.' Janat, Haseeb and Usman were all in the same cage, two in front of the dead Giorgio's cage. When they got near the ground, they jumped out and when Giorgio's cage came by, they grabbed the package.

The skywheel had stopped but the cages with the Spiders were still at the top. The Iranians opened fire on Tuppence, so she was down behind a large model of Cinderella, and when the firing stopped, they were gone. By the time the police arrived, the Spiders were also gone.

The Iranian took the package back to their hotel.

When they opened it, There was a picture of a skull and crossbones and the words 'Respiration warning: masks must be worn', and five plastic all-in-one suits from head to toe were also in the package.

Janat said, 'Hey, what are these five capsules?'

They didn't need to know what they were, but they knew it was very bad stuff. But where was the FLC?

Janat said, 'We may not have what we came for, but I bet the government will pay big money for these.'

The ASIO and MI6 had not released any details of the coronavirus germs in the ampoules for fear of public panic, and Ziggy hadn't been able to contact Nadia or Giorgio, so he was worrying where the ampoules were. The Spiders decided to go back to the hotel where Nadia was staying and get into her room. Maybe they would learn where the package was going before it was stolen by the Iranians.

When they walked into the foyer, Tuppence said, 'Shit! There they are.'

The three Iranians were getting into the lift, and Haseeb was carrying a small satchel bag just the right size for the FLC.

Brewster said, 'We can't do much here. We should wait outside and follow them for a better opportunity.'

Slowpoke said, 'Here they come. I wonder where they parked their camels.'

They followed them to a small airport thirty-five kilometres out of Rome and waited while the Iranians went into a building with a sign, 'Aircraft hire'. When they left, the Spiders went in and asked what aircraft were for hire and they hoped that the people who'd just left hadn't hired the last one.

'No,' they said, 'they are flying tomorrow at 8 am and have hired for the day a Robinson 44 Raven.

The Spiders said, 'Thank you', and left.

They drove down to another building that said HeliVenture Hire. Wiggy provided them with his licence and they booked a six-seater Eurocopter for 8 am the next day.

When they got back out to the car, Auntie said, 'Shit, Wiggy, can you fly?'

'I guess we will find out tomorrow, won't we?'

'Jesus, you're kidding!' they all said.

Wiggy said, 'We don't know where they're going so I can't log a flight plan. That means we will be flying by visual flight rules (VFR) instead of instrument flight rules (IFR).'

The next day, they followed the Iranians to the airport and watched them park and walk to the Robinson R44. The Spiders drove on to HeliVenture and their Eurocopter. Wiggy did his external and internal preflight checks, and went through the start-up routine. The main rotors and tail rotor were operating, and all the instruments were good. They were ready to lift off when they saw the Iranians leaving.

Wiggy said, 'I suppose this is not a good time to tell you I haven't flown for a long time, and I've never flown one of these things.'

The girls all said they wanted to get out; the boys weren't all that keen either.

'Too late,' Wiggy said, 'There they go.'

So, up the Spiders went into the bright blue yonder. It was a bloody awful, shaky lift-off with the chopper swaying from side to side and up and down, but it didn't take long for Wiggy to get it all together. His passengers started to relax and accused him of doing the rough lift-off on purpose just to scare them, because that's exactly the sort of thing he would do. What they didn't know was that was one of his better lift-offs. They were flying south-west from Rome above the Tyrrhenian Sea in the direction of the Isle of Capri with the radar showing the Iranians 2000 metres ahead. Wiggy knew the Robby wouldn't have the equipment the airbus Eurocopter had, so the Iranians wouldn't know they were there as long as they stayed where they were. Using Capri as a destination for now, their instruments told them the flight time was twenty minutes. There wasn't much talking among the Spiders; they were probably busy praying or shitting their pants, and if Max hadn't been flying, he would have been doing the same.

The island came into view with its high cliffs and rocky outcrops. Wiggy banked the chopper north and raised the altitude so the Iranians wouldn't see them when they turned to land. They must have had a set of binoculars because they banked as well and were coming to see who they were.

Slim said, 'Open the two side doors, Wiggy. Everybody, lie flat on the floor – Brewster and Auntie on one side and Slim and Slowpoke on the other. Tuppence is up in the cockpit with Wiggy. When they get here, Wiggy, swing us side on.'

Wiggy said, 'Let me know when your guns are empty, and I'll go up over the top of him and Brewster and Auntie can have a go.'

The Iranians flew in close and suddenly realised who they were too late. The seven Ps of prior preparation and planning gave the Spiders the upper hand. They pumped twenty-four rounds into one side of the Robby. Slim called out, 'Up now, Wiggy,' and the chopper went up and over the Robby after several ups, downs and sideways manoeuvres with, at one stage, the rotor blades almost touching. The two Iranians in the back were dead and Janat was flying.

Slim called out, 'Don't both shoot at the same bloody thing. Brewster, you get the pilot. Auntie, you get the fuel tank – it's full of Jet A-1 fuel.'

She said, 'Where's that?'

'Jesus,' said Wiggy, 'that black round thing on the back.'

Slim had reloaded by now, so he pounded it as well. It didn't take long before the tank erupted and down went the Robby into the ocean with three dead Iranians. They banked around several times in a circle down low.

Slowpoke said, 'What's that satchel thing floating down there near the wreckage?'

Wiggy took the chopper down and hovered a foot off the water. (Well, every now and then, it was two feet, but he was doing his best.) Brewster hung out over the skids and grabbed the satchel, then they flew off in the direction of the island.

'Well,' said Tuppence, 'we are about to see what all the dead bodies have been about. I think you will be right, Slim – there won't be any FLCs in the bag ... Shit, what are these things?'

'Whatever they are, they're bad news,' Auntie said.

There was a note in the satchel that read 'Cockleshell needs a friend'.

'What does that mean?' they all said.

'Alpha Charlie Bravo Capri Tower, this is Helicopter Mike Charlie Alpha 468 inbound from Rome. Permission and clearance to land. Over.'

'Mike Charlie Alpha, approach from the north to the General Aviation Area. Report on landing.'

They rang CIA to bring them up to date.

'Where are you now? Are you still on the island? Do not go anywhere that package and guard it with your lives. We will be there within the hour.'

There were four of them from CIA and MI6, two from each department. The head honcho and his little honcho were ecstatic about what they had done and made it sound like they had saved the world. They said it was a shame they were so old as they would have made good agents.

Slowpoke said, 'What do you mean, "would have"? What do you think we've been doing? How do you think you've got what's in your hand, young whippersnapper? While you've been polishing the seat of your pants, we've been bloody shot at and threatened, you cheeky bugger.'

They told the Spiders what was in the ampoules and that there were supposedly another five of them at Lakes Entrance. Nitro and Sparkie had been asked to help. They knew that because they were staying at Fairview.

'You people can all go home now. We will make sure your expenses are paid quickly for you, and someone will be in touch before you get home.'

'Not so fast,' said Auntie, 'You people are buying dinner, and we'll pick the restaurant. They chose La Palette and drank the most expensive wine they had.'

'Let's go home,' Wiggy said, 'I'm tired, I'm sore and I'm buggered. You can only squeeze so much from one lemon, especially an old one, and we've all been squeezed dry.'

* * *

When Lilly opened the small package and saw what was in it, she didn't know what they were, but she knew they would be bad news, and worth a lot of money on the black market. She didn't feel safe now, so she left the package in Post Office Box 841 at Lakes Entrance and flew back to Mexico, and she would send the PO Box key to the highest bidder when she was safely home. She would also give the authorities enough information to arrest Ziggy, if he hadn't been found out already. Lily might not have been the most honest person in the world, but she was not a mass murderer.

Chapter 9

Christmas had come and gone. They had communicated with families by phone on Christmas Day from where they were, which meant they had needed to invent an incredible amount of bullshit as to why they were not home with their families on that one day of the year that most people were.

It was now July. On their last leg home, flying from Sydney to Melbourne with Qantas, there was a spare seat next to Tuppence on the aisle. Thirty minutes into the flight, a man took up the seat, unfolded a newspaper and began reading.

When the drink trolley arrived, he said, 'What would you like to drink, Tuppence? And what about you, Wiggy?'

'I'm sorry,' Wiggy said, 'you have the wrong people.'

'I don't think so,' he said. 'We all had a lovely holiday on Last Chance Island. I'm Lieutenant Commander Harrigan.'

'You don't look anything like Harrigan,' Wiggy said.

'Well, that's the idea, Wiggy, isn't it? We only have an hour left of the flight, so I won't waste time on idle chitchat. ASIO has intelligence that a small package, which we believe holds another five ampoules, the same as the ampoules that you retrieved and handed over, have now been delivered by a courier to Lakes Entrance in Victoria.'

'Yes, we heard that,' said Wiggy.

'Right. We want the Spiders to help us again. You will be given ID cards that will overrule any other authority here in Australia that hinders your investigation.'

Wiggy said, 'If Nitro and Sparkie are in, it'll be all in as usual. Have you spoken to the others here on this plane as well? Harrigan said "I know they're on the plane because we're paying for it.'

'And so you bloody well should,' said Wiggy.'

'Well, yes, we should,' he said, 'No need to throw the toys out of the cot, Wiggy. I have spoken to them, and they said one in, all in.'

When they got home, the neighbours said, 'Did you have a nice holiday? Sometimes it's good to get away from all the stress and worry and come home nice and relaxed.'

Max and Jane just looked at each other and started laughing.

Everyone went home to unpack and feed the fish (Wiggy doubted that Auntie's fish would still be alive) and then they would be back at Fairview in two days for a meeting.

* * *

Back in Mexico, Lilly put the prearranged, coded message on the dark web for the pick-up of the package along with the number 841. She had no knowledge of the chips sold to the Iranians that the Spiders thought didn't exist, that they had been scammed out of $250 million, and that they also knew about a package supposedly at Lakes Entrance, so they would presumably be visiting Lakes Entrance as well. Who knows how the people who live and survive in the evil world find things out?

There was a knock. Lilly opened the door. There were two men with fur trapper hats, or ushankas as they're known in Russia, with the side flaps pulled down and tied around their chins. They pulled her out by the hair and into a car. She knew it would be about the package at Lakes Entrance. Once you use the dark web, it attracts the scumbags who don't play fair, and that's what this was.

They said, 'We want to know where the package with the microchips is. Is it still in Lakes Entrance, and if so, where exactly?'

She said, 'I don't know anything about microchips. The package in Lakes Entrance has little bottle things in it. It's not for you, it's for someone else, and I don't know who that is either.'

'That is not the information we have. So, last chance – where is the package?'

She said, 'You're a dumb bastard, aren't you? You don't get it. I don't know anything about microchips.'

They drove her to the airport where a helicopter was waiting. They pushed her in and lifted off. At about nine hundred metres, they tied her feet together and her hands behind her back, hooked her onto the winch and pushed her out. The winch was played out till she was about seven metres under the chopper, hanging upside down and being dragged through the air by her feet. After twenty minutes of hanging there, the winch pulled her back into the chopper. Her nose was bleeding freely.

'Where are the microchips?' they said.

She knew she was dead anyway.

'They don't exist, but if they did, they would probably be with all the other mail. Now, go and get stuffed.'

As they pushed her out minus the winch cable, she smiled and called out, 'Hey, dickhead, you don't have the number.'

The Russians were instructed to go back home. They were sending someone else to Lakes Entrance. They would have to wait and see who picked up the package because they didn't have a mailbox number or a key.

*   *   *

The Spiders were all together again at Fairview, sitting around the fire with a red wine.

'I want to go back to using real names,' said Brewster.

'Well, if you're coming with us, you can't. We are stuck with them while we're on this case,' said Slim, 'and by the way, Wiggy, you didn't tell any of us you could fly a helicopter.'

'I've only got a baby licence. Back here in Australia, I wouldn't be allowed to fly that particular one.'

'Yeah, well, you scared the pants off us, Max.'

'You're still here, though, aren't you?'

'Enough of the reminiscing. How are we going to play this?' Tuppence said. 'First, we need to find the person who bought it here or where they have hidden it for safekeeping. I don't think they would be walking around with the package on their person. They are my comments to get the meeting off to a start.'

Slowpoke said, 'Lakes Entrance isn't that big. I don't understand why this package is even here. If they were planning for a large saturation of germs, you would hardly do it here. The Southern Cross train station at peak hour would be the more likely the place. No, I don't think anything is going to happen here. I think this is just a stepping stone for something else. There's a lot of stuff we don't know about or are not being told about: microchips that never existed and were only a smokescreen for something else, the capsules we recovered and now these ones. Where did they come from? Who do they belong to and who wants to get them back? Is it our dumb mob, or someone else's? You can bet your nuts, boys, there will be other interested parties. While I'm thinking about all this, and before I forget, make sure your cars are packed ready to go at a moment's notice, with chains on in case we go into the mountains. I have packed the Land Cruiser ute with ration packs, water and a small amount of firewood. If we don't need it, I'll just unpack it. Remember the seven Ps. There are only four places they can stay here in Lakes – hotels, motels, apartments and caravan parks – but that's the last place I would look.

'Good,' said Auntie. 'Someone, impress me with how we find them and who they are, given that they are just ghosts now.'

'That's a very good question. Would somebody like to come forward with the answer to that?' said Nitro.

'There are several hire car places at Tullamarine Airport. I suggest our friend Harrigan checks if anyone hired a car and made a comment that they were going to Lakes Entrance. If they come by bus, we can't trace them,' said Sparkie.

Wiggy said, 'I'll talk to Harrigan. One consolation is it's not Christmas when there's another twenty-five thousand people here.'

When he spoke to Harrigan, he told Wiggy that his top

agents had passed on to their opponents in Iran that the microchips had been recovered so they could go back home.

Slim said he would visit all the motels to find out if people were or had been staying there with an overseas address. Nitro and Brewster would do the same at the hotels, apartments and caravan parks. Mind you, this was only any good if they had come from overseas; they might be an Australian, although that was doubtful. Wiggy would deal with Harrigan and see what came of that. Now that they had their special ID Cards, they shouldn't have a problem getting any information they wanted.

Slim trudged around all the motels in town with no luck. The Bellevue on the Lakes was the last one on his list. The owner said she wasn't giving Slim any information, even if he showed her a card to fly to the moon. Slim had to get the police to come to the motel. When she was told she would be going to jail, she became a different person. Slim went through the books for who was currently there and who had stayed there. The only one who stood out was a Lilly Hernandez from Durango in Mexico, but she had left two days ago after a four-week stay. Slim said thanks and left.

The other Spiders had all drawn a blank. Slim gave the gang what he had found.

Wiggy said, 'Remarkably interesting, Slim. Harrigan's information is a woman arrived in Australia four weeks ago from Durango in Mexico, hired a black Jaguar F-Pace SUV and two days ago flew out of Tullamarine back to Mexico.'

'She was probably here for a holiday,' said Auntie.

'Don't be ridiculous,' Brewster said, 'Who the hell comes from Mexico for a holiday at Lakes Entrance? Anyone got any ideas? So, what's the go, then? If she was the courier, did she take the package back to Mexico? I don't think so. Did she leave it here for someone to pick up, or as Auntie said, was she on holidays? Not likely. There's nothing to keep anyone here in Lakes Entrance for four week, particularly if you've flown all the way from Mexico. She has got to have been the courier.'

'Right,' said Tuppence, 'everyone put yourself in her place. What would you do if you wanted to leave something here for pick up at a later date? Where would you put a small package to keep it safe?'

'Well,' said Sparkie, 'I would give it to a solicitor to hold, or she might have befriended someone to keep it for her.'

'No,' said Wiggy, 'I think she knows what's in the package and she wouldn't just give it to someone she only met for a couple of weeks. What about you, Nitro? What would you do?'

'Buggered if I know,' he said. 'I would probably rent a Post Office Box, depending on how small this package is.'

'Jesus, you're a bloody genius, Nitro! We have her name so in the morning, it's post office, here we come.'

The next morning, Slim and Slowpoke dressed in their business clothes and asked for the manager of the post office. They told her only what they had to and gave her Lilly's details. She checked with the local police who advised her everything was above board. They were taken into the sorting room where mail was placed in the open boxes on this side, and there in Box number 841 was a small black satchel that you could tell had been opened because the number lock had been forced open.

Slim said, 'We want you to put a cover over this box. On

this side, no more mail to go into the box and no one to touch the box.'

They went outside and rang Harrigan.

He said, 'Wait and watch for whoever comes to get it and follow them.'

'Jesus, Wiggy said, 'just come and get the bloody thing, and it's all over!'

'Can't do that. We need to know where it's going and with who.'

The Spiders didn't fancy having to sit in a car at the post boxes for who knew how long, so they had the key slot mechanism changed so whoever was coming would have to go into the post office to pick up the package and the post office would ring the Spiders who were only ten minutes away.

'Well, here we go again,' Slim said. 'We don't know who they are, what they look like or where they're from, so nothing's changed as I see it, but I bet we find out all of that very soon.'

* * *

As soon as the information hit the dark web, the Russians were right on to it, and so was the party that had been waiting for it to come online once they had received the code that pick-up was ready at Lakes Entrance. They would need to wait till the PO Box key arrived from Lilly before they left. A new set of Russians was still looking for a package somewhere in Rome, and now they needed to send agents to Lakes Entrance as well to watch who picked up the package. The Russians who were sent to Australia were Natasha Petrova and Alexey Volcov who were now on their way in a silver Ford Ranger hire car.

*   *   *

The next day, Slowpoke and Auntie needed stamps. They had parked the car in the side street next to the post office, and when they turned the corner, Auntie said, 'My God, look at that!' On the other side of the road was, well, the only way to explain it was a half man, half woman, at least six feet tall with lots of facial hair who looked like she could kill somebody with her little finger – except she didn't have any fingers.

The woman had no hands. There were couplings with a ratchet locking device implanted into the ends of her arms, where she could click in a variety of implements specifically designed to lock into place, like a knife, and fork, a claw grab and lock device, fittings with pens and pencils and a large, long, vicious looking corkscrew – the list was endless. One small twist and they unlocked. She certainly had the look of a bad arse person, and that was confirmed when they heard her say to the man with her, 'Look how this bastard parked their car. I should wait here and dispose of them and do the town a favour.' She was carrying a shoulder bag which obviously held all the devices she could click into her arms.

'I wonder who she is. I bet she's not a local. She had a European accent.'

The man with her was of average height with the sort of cauliflower ears that wrestlers get. His nose had been broken at least once. He had green eyes and a thin wispy mouth that said, you'd be a fool to trust me.

When they got back to Fairview and told the other Spiders what they had seen, Slim said, 'Looks like the first of the partygoers have arrived. We should start blowing up the balloons and loading our party bang-bangs.'

'Okay,' Wiggy said, 'before this gets out of hand again – and it will – let's sit down and try and put all this together. So, brains switched on, everyone. Let's go right back to the start.'

'I'll start,' said Auntie. 'We were watching, on Last Chance Island, for the transfer of microchips in a package which we now know, or think we know, never existed.'

Slim cut in. 'Russia, the dark web and Iran were in the chase all over Europe for the package. The Iranians had paid big money for the chips but never got them, so they weren't going away.'

Nitro said, 'What if it's our government that's pulling the strings on all of this? Nobody ever saw the microchips, did they, but someone wanted everyone out there chasing a package with nothing in it. Then suddenly there's two packages containing ampoules of deadly toxins. Now, don't tell me we have seen them, because we haven't. We've only seen little glass things with liquid in them, and the way all this cloak-and-dagger shit has been going on, how do you know they're not just full of water?'

'Well, if you're right,' said Tuppence, 'there's a lot of dead bodies for imaginary microchips and ten ampoules of water.'

'Or maybe,' said Slim, 'originally there were the chips back on Last Chance Island and the dark web got Iran's money and the chips, and then led everyone to believe the chips were still in the package to keep the Iranians off their back. Just between you and me, I think what we're doing now is a separate issue all together. And what about that note that said, "Cockleshell needs a friend"?'

Slim's phone rang. It was Lyn at the post office.

'They're here. They are wearing grey suits with a medical

snake and staff pin in their lapels. I will stall them as long as I can, then give them the package.'

Wiggy said, 'Tuppence and I will go first. Last one out makes sure everything's off and locks the house. We will stay in touch by phone and keep swapping the car that is tailing. That's four different cars – they'll never pick that.'

When they got to the post office, the blokes in the suits were just coming out carrying the package. They drove off towards Bairnsdale in a Toyota Combi Van and took the turn off to Bruthen. Wiggy stayed way back. He knew where the road went, and he rang the other Spiders and told them where they were, and where they were probably going. If it was Mount Hotham, they'd better have snow chains, or they won't going to be allowed through.

Wiggy said to Tuppence, 'I keep telling everyone about the seven Ps – prior preparation and planning prevents piss poor performance – but nobody listens. Slim just tells me I sound like a broken record.'

Slim and Slowpoke were tailing the car now.

She called Wiggy and said, 'The silver Ford Ranger that just passed us has that woman in it that has no hands, and the slimy looking bloke s driving.'

Chapter 10

The two Russians, Natasha and Alexey decided, they would probably need snow chains.

'Next town we can hire them. Map says, Bruthen, fifty-eight kilometres. We are on the Great Alpine Road so if we stop, we won't lose them.'

When Brewster and Auntie's Chrysler 300 pulled over across from the Ford Ranger in Bruthen, Brewster said, 'Shit!'

'Yes, that's her,' said Auntie.'

'Jesus, I hope she never comes near any of us!'

They watched as the other cars drove by and found a place to stop. It appeared that those who hadn't had chains now did. They made sure the Ford Ranger was the first car behind the Combi' that way they knew where the enemy was. Nitro and Sparkie's was the tail car. The typical High Country curves, twists, valleys, and climbs slowed the travel down.

Up ahead there was a police roadblock, and cars were being sent off to the left onto a rest area. The sign read: 'Black ice over road. Road closed. Open 10 am tomorrow. Chains must be on. $300 fine. Forty kilometres per hour.'

The police said, 'Stay here tonight or turn back: your

choice. We'll will be here all night for the roadblock, so you would be safe staying.'

'If the police see her, this female werewolf,' Wiggy said, 'I bet they wouldn't be keen to stay the night. There are lots of cars here going to the snow and we will be seen as one of them, so amble over here and get a ration pack and a sleeping bag if you want one to keep you warm in the car. If I were you, I would be putting the snow chains on now in case it's snowing tomorrow. It's up to you, your choice.'

As everyone came over to the ute, Wiggy told them to stay in touch over the phones during the night, 'But don't talk them flat. They are our only ways of communicating to each other and the outside world.'

The night was uneventful, and the cars started feeding their way out on to the highway at about 10 am. It was Wiggy and Tuppence's turn as the tail car. They sat back six or seven cars from the HiAce van, they noticed the silver Ford Ranger was right behind the van.

Arriving at Mount Hotham, the cars started dispersing in all directions. The Spiders followed the van and the Ranger to the main chalet and waited outside for the two suits and the driver of the Ranger to come out.

'I can understand why she didn't go in,' said Brewster. 'The Russians, if that's who they are, didn't actually book in. They were there just keeping tabs on the two suits.'

They gave them five minutes before they went in.

The lady at the counter said, 'Do you have a booking?'

'No, we don't,' said Slim.

'Well, I'm sorry, we are booked out.'

'What about our friends? Did they get in?'

'No, but they're staying at the Cockleshell Cabins about

ten kilometres into the hills. I can give you a bunk house that sleeps eight people. Two of the cabins, numbers 1 and 2 are privately owned. You will all be in cabin 5. At this stage, you will be the only ones there and it's very private. You will need to hire four snowmobiles to get you to Cockleshell, and I wouldn't wait too long as there is a snowstorm coming. You can hire the snow scooters behind the building.'

When they got outside, Tuppence said, 'Remember the note in the bag that said something about Cockleshell?'

The signposts were pretty good, but the falling snow was quickly covering up the tracks of the snow scooters in front of them and vision was getting worse. So, they hooked up a tarpaulin to some suitable trees they found and set up their small one-man tents under it. Remembering the seven Ps, Wiggy had given them their ration packs, and each snow scooter had been loaded with firewood. The fire was going, the billy was boiling and they were fairly well sheltered under the tarpaulin, but it was still bloody cold, and they wondered if the others had got through before the storm.

Slim said, 'They haven't got the equipment we have got. If they didn't get through, they will all be dead by morning.'

The storm was relatively small and while it wasn't five-star accommodation, they did get some sleep. The next morning, they packed up and headed towards the cabins.

About a kilometre along the track, Slowpoke said to Slim on their scooter, 'There's someone standing next to a tree up ahead.'

As they got closer, they could see it was one of the suits.

Tuppence said, 'I spy with my little eye something beginning with D for "dead".'

He had been tied to a tree and his hands had been cut

off. A long corkscrew was sticking out of the top of his head. His eyeballs, the same colour and size as the marbles Wiggy played with at school, had come right out of their sockets and were hanging down his face on two thin pieces of sinew. The force of the corkscrew being thrust up from under his jaw had shot his tongue out and the pressure of it ramming into his brain had shot the eyeballs out of their sockets. There were no prizes for guessing who was responsible for this. She was what you paid for to see behind bars at a circus, and as a kid, you poked your tongue out at her because you knew she couldn't get out, and then went home and had nightmares.

Number 5 cabin was far enough away from the other cabins for them to arrive without being seen, or so they thought. They were still unpacking when there was a knock on the door. Slim said he would get it. He took the safety off his gun and held the gun behind his back. He opened the door to find the slimy dude standing there.

He said, 'Hello.'

Slim said, 'Goodbye', and shot him between the eyes.

'Jesus,' Wiggy said, 'what did you do that for?'

'I got tired of waiting for them to kill us.'

'You've got no bloody patience, Slim.'

Brewster said, 'I guess the band has arrived, so let the dancing begin.'

The werewolf woman came out of the cabin to see where the bag with the package was and grabbed hold of the steel railings around the veranda with her claw. It went 'click' and froze from the cold. She tried to unfasten it with no luck. She tried to twist it off her arm but that was also affected by the cold, so she was stuck there.

Slim danced around in front of her, yelling out, 'Yeah,

come on, have a go, you shithead. Have a go. Come on, I can take you', and he poked her with the stick.

Brewster said, 'If she gets the claw free, you'd better be a long way from here, Slim. Look at that carving knife she's got on the other arm – she will carve you up to nothing. Come away. We are all going inside to find the other suit.'

Slim shot the werewolf woman in both kneecaps. 'Just in case you get free,' he said and went in with the others.

The place was covered in blood. The suit's head was in the kitchen sink, the rest of him was sitting on a chair and both his hands had been cut off. The Spiders still didn't know who they were or whose side they were on, but they certainly had something to do with the government by the medical lapel badges they were wearing.

They gave the cabins a thorough going-over. In one particular cupboard that Nitro and Tuppence checked were two switches, green for open and a red for close. They pressed the green one and a motorised noise came from somewhere in the lounge and kitchen area. A floor panel opened up from under the floor mat, which was now down the hole. A set of stairs appeared, and lights came on with the stairs. The Spiders couldn't believe what they were seeing.

One by one, they went down. The room was the same size as the one above it. There were rows of sliding cabinets with hundreds of bottles of medicines, and more shelves full of vials and ampoules and an enormous number of drugs of all varieties. They could keep all this stuff down there because it was a cool room made by nature – very clever.

Wiggy rang Harrigan at ASIS, who said, 'Shit, unbelievable! We will be there in an hour.'

Wiggy said, 'Don't go to the chalet. We are at the Cockleshell cabins ten kilometres west behind the chalet.'

They followed a passageway to another set of stairs, with motion-activated lights. Although the trap door above was locked, they could tell it went to cabin number two. The room they now stood in was a duplicate of the first one, but the steel cabinets here were more like a locker for storage of clothes, and there were six of them. Slowpoke opened the first one and a female body fell out.

'Jesus,' she said, 'I'm going to have nightmares for the rest of my life. I can't believe we are all doing this stuff at our age.'

As it turned out, there were three more bodies in the lockers. There were also two keys on the floor of the locker the dead woman was in, which Tuppence picked up and put in her pocket.

'What was that noise? Auntie said, 'Sounded like something falling downstairs.'

They all went to look.

'Shit,' Brewster said. 'It's that bloody woman! She has crawled down here after being shot in the kneecaps. She must have been able to free herself.'

She was frothing at the mouth and screaming in what was definitely Russian, pointing at Slim and yelling, 'I kill, I kill you, bastard!'

Brewster said, 'Christ, I can't put up with this anymore. You probably had a lousy young life without hands, and this is what's happened to you. So I'll do you a favour.'

He shot her three times. They could hear a helicopter coming. When it touched down, Special Forces soldiers jumped out along with Harrigan and a couple of his followers.

He said, 'You old buggers are unbelievable!'

They took him into the cabin, and they did a walk-through of what had happened. Because of what was found below the cabin with the bodies, it was decided to break in and check it out.

The inside of the cabin was identical to the others, except this one also had a trap door under the carpet like next door. This kitchen also had blood everywhere, and small pieces of body parts such as fingers and ears and a complete left hand were in the kitchen sink. When they checked the bathroom, they found the rest of the body minus the head. A uniform and workshirt were hanging on the doorknob. The badge said, 'Mount Hotham Ranger'. The police found his snowmobile at the back of the cabin.

Nitro said, 'Do you think the woman with no hands had enough time to do all this?'

'We weren't all that far behind her,' said Tuppence. 'Maybe it was done by whoever did the job on the ones in the lockers down those stairs.'

'Maybe,' said Slim, 'but I bet it's all got to do with the bloody microchips or the ampoules. We are not being told things and that amounts to lying by omission, which is just straight out lying. The deception we have had with who's who and which package is which has been bloody deplorable, to say the least.'

Harrigan said, 'Some of it we didn't know ourselves, and some of it was covered by national security. There was a risk to public safety with some of the information that we had.'

'Well,' Wiggy said, 'I have had to listen to a load of cover-up bullshit in twenty years in the service, and you, Harrigan, are right up there with it. There's a library in Canberra and in there, there must be a section, probably next to the fiction, with a sign that says, "Government bullshit section: stories, speeches and excuses for all occasions, books not to leave the library due to high demand".'

After that little outburst, Harrigan promised to tell them from start to finish what it had all been about.

'And not before time,' said Slowpoke. 'We will be waiting with bated breath.'

The police had been and gone, and the bodies had been removed, so everyone sat round Harrigan. It reminded Tuppence of when she was a kid and everyone sat round Dad while he told a story.

She said, 'I'll start it for you if you like. Once upon a time, there were eight elderly Spiders ...'

Harrigan said, 'Do you want to hear this or not? If I gave you every little detail, I would have to write a book, but I'll give you enough to fill in the gaps of what you already know.

'Someone had been stealing drugs, toxins and other important medical serums and ampoules from the government laboratories here in Victoria. We tracked it down to one man (his name is not important) who worked there, and we waited for his next move. A man called Ziggy Oliver had embezzled a huge sum of money from a financial services company when he was their assistant manager. He was jailed for ten years but has now been released. We thought he wanted the money for drugs because he was a junkie, so we took a chance and put our own man in the laboratory and a stoolie agent in the cell with Ziggy who told him he knew someone who could get him as many drugs as he wanted. Ziggy apparently didn't want drugs for himself; he wanted revenge on the world. He wanted ampoules of toxin. We asked the laboratory to make up ten ampoules containing water which we let Ziggy steal which he gave to a courier to deliver. Our package was now out there with the microchips package. We were happy to let it all roll on, waiting to see where the ampoules were going. The two suits, as you have been calling them, were government heads and responsible for the movement of restricted and for-your-eyes-only parcels and correspondence who obviously had been caught up in this drug ring.

'Now this is where it gets tricky. At the same time CIA was organising the bait for the drugs, MI6 told them of the microchips heading for Australia so Warrant Officer Shepherd came up with the suggestion to use retirees – that's you, the not-so-old-in-smarts sitting here. The microchips were stolen by the dark web along with Iran's $250 million during the handover on Last Chance Island, and now the Iranians were after the package or their money which was rightfully theirs, but no one knew there were now two packages out there.

'We have the microchips safely in our possession, unless there really are two sets. We have the drugs and who was stealing them, so that should have been the end. But now we have these bodies to contend with: two men and two women aged somewhere in their forties who haven't been in the lockers for more than three months, according to the medical examiner from the coroner's office. Now before I ask you ...'

'No, you don't,' said Wiggy, 'We are finished. We have done our bit for king and country. It's time for us to go home.'

'Well, that's your choice, of course,' said Harrigan, 'but give me a chance to tell my side. Our top agents in the ASIS earn $1500 a week. If you stay on for this last mission, we will give you your own ASIS identification, Slowpoke will get her old one back, and you would be paid as an agent at $1500 a week, with backpay from December. That's eight months' pay totalling $48,000 to date – but only if you stay to help finish the case.'

Slowpoke could just see herself walking the golf course with the latest upmarket golf clubs, new buggy and golf shoes, along with anything else Drummond Golf had that took her fancy.

'When you think about it,' she said, 'we have actually already earned this money, so it's not such a good deal. We're actually being held to ransom, which doesn't surprise me with our government.'

They all agreed they wanted the money, but it was a shabby way these bastards were doing it. They agreed to stay only as long as it took to sort out the drama with the bodies.

Tuppence said, 'We're not lifting a finger till our backpay money is in the bank. I know how slow this government works when it comes to giving people money.'

It was time to go home and tend to the outside maintenance, see family and friends, and so on, but they had to sign the Secrecy Act, so any discussion as to their activities were off limits. They all agreed to meet again in two weeks for a plan for the mystery bodies.

* * *

Wiggy and Tuppence had been home a couple of days when Jane found two keys in her pocket, the ones from the bottom of the locker with the dead woman she had forgotten about.

Max said, 'When the others get here, we can check the numbers on the keys and go from there. One of them looks like a house key and the other a car key, although car keys now just have a key fob.'

One by one, the group arrived back at Fairview, and once again, the boys burned the steak. After the barbecue, they sat around and spoke about the mystery bodies and where and how to begin. The bodies had no form of ID, so how hard this was going to be.

Tuppence told the group about the two keys she had found. They rang a locksmith and gave him the numbers on the keys. He told them one was someone's Yale front door key and the other was for a 1990 Mazda 626. They went to the police with the information, as they had to find out what they did with unclaimed cars. They were given the names of the eight storage facilities that store abandoned cars until claimed or auctioned. Cars that have not moved for two months are considered abandoned and are towed away.

Based on the medical examiner's information, the bodies had been there for three or four months, so if the car had been on the street for that long, there was a chance it had been towed away to one of the facilities the police had given them.

These facilities were across all of Melbourne, so they all agreed to stay in Melbourne for the next couple of nights. All those who lived in the suburbs agreed to stay in a motel so they would be together, and anyway the government would be paying. Everyone chose a facility to check in the morning.

Tuppence arrived at Private Stack Storage in South Melbourne and spoke to the manager who, as expected in a place like this, was rude and a stand-over merchant.

He said, 'Piss off, lady. Don't think you can just come here and tell me what you want.'

She showed him her ASIS ID and said, 'If I were you, I

would go home and pack some clothes. When the police get here, you, mister, will be going to jail.'

'Whoa, hang on, lady. I didn't know who you were.'

'Well, you do now, so get your arse out of the office and help. Have you got a car fitting this description?'

'I don't know.'

'I will go with you, and we will look.'

'There's a Mazda 626 over there.'

Tuppence put the key in the ignition. It couldn't quite start the car as the battery was too low, but, yes, this was definitely the right car. In the glove box was the owner's service book and registration papers. The owner's name was Fiona Webster, and she lived at Parky Place, Cottage Road, Greensand. What a lucky break!

Tuppence said to the manager, 'Thanks, and try not to be such a bully and a prick. Practise being a nice prick or I'll come back and have the place closed on health grounds. So, play nice with everyone.'

Tuppence gave Fiona's address to the other Spiders to all meet there in an hour's time. The key opened the front door and in they went. It was a neat and tidy two-bedroom apartment, and you could tell immediately a woman lived here by herself. They spread out and searched the house for more clues.

Slim called out, 'Hey, come and have a look at this.'

When they came into the bedroom, he showed them letters and correspondence that addressed her as Dr Fiona Webster, Neurology Surgeon, West Bank Brain Clinic.

'Jesus,' Slowpoke said, 'is everyone thinking what I'm thinking? Cast your mind back to the FLC chips which Harrigan tells us is in our government's possession. How does that work, because these people were getting ready to implant the chip into someone's brain as soon as they got their hands on the package. See, there is correspondence written to three others – another doctor and two anaesthetists – and I'll bet they are the other three bodies we found at Mount Hotham. Well, that's someone else's problem. What I want to know is, what were they doing at Mount Hotham in a hideout for drugs like the ampoules, nothing to do with the FLC chips. What were they all doing up there?'

The front doorbell rang. They all looked at each other.

Brewster said, 'Well, someone see who it is and invite them in, whether they want to or not.'

Slowpoke said she would go. When she opened the door, a woman was standing there, who said, 'You're not Fiona! Who are you?"

Slowpoke grabbed her by the hair, hauled her inside and shut the door. They sat her down, showed her their ID and said, 'We need some answers.'

'Fiona is dead? Oh, shit,' she said. 'I was just going to be the contract theatre sister for the operation. I haven't done anything wrong. I came here today to pick up my contract payment. They left me a message that they had done the operation and didn't need me but they would pay me anyway.'

'What was the operation?'

'A frontal lobe tissue repair and realignment. It had to be done in a cold environment at Mount Hotham. They had rented a cabin somewhere up there and were waiting for the arrival of a package with a piece of equipment needed for the operation and I would be notified the day before the operation. But I have not heard from Fiona. The whole thing seemed very strange, but they paid me a lot of money for the job. I needed the money, so I said I would assist at the operation.'

'Well, you're an incredibly lucky young lady, because had you got involved, you would have been dead five minutes after the operation, like the four who did the operation, or else killed today when you came for your money. You won't be arrested but we need your details in case we need to talk to you again.'

When she left, Wiggy said, 'Smart-arse Harrigan and his mob ASIS don't have any idea what's going on. There must be a second set of microchips and someone's walking around with them in his or her head. I bet that lights up the ASIO, CIA AND MI6 world. Who wants the joy of giving Harrigan this latest information?'

Tuppence volunteered. She told him all about the car, the house and the theatre sister's account of what has happened.

Harrigan said, 'We were initially told there *could* have been a second chip, but we had no knowledge of its whereabouts, or even if there was another chip. Well, now you know there is, and it's walking around in someone's head. That's not good news, so we want you to send a Spider to London for a meeting with MI6. A ticket will be at the Qantas terminal, and I will meet him or her at the airport in London. So who will be going?'

They said it would be Nitro.

After the meeting in London, he rang the Spiders and gave them all the information discussed at the meeting.

'What a bloody eye-opener that was!' he said. 'ASIO and the Americans have to have their bloody doughnuts and coffee and the English their cups of tea and scones before they do anything. Then the bullshit starts. One mob says, we can't do it like that because some other department will get their nose out of joint, then the other mob says they're not happy either because it's winter and they haven't been given their new jackets yet. No wonder nothing gets done!'

The Spiders reminded him they were on standby to go if asked, and Brewster reminded them all that those bastards had taken over their lives. He wondered if there would ever be an end to it all.

Chapter 11

When Nitro got off the plane in Melbourne, there was a man holding up a sign that said, 'Car for Nitro.' He was a commonwealth driver sent to deliver him to a meeting.

Fair enough, thought Nitro and left with the man. He wasn't concerned where the meeting was being held until they stopped at a building that said 'Bones Meat Factory, enter through side door, deliveries at the rear'.

The driver drew his gun and said, 'Get out. And no talking on the way, or I'll shoot you where you stand. Makes no difference to me.'

Once inside, they walked past dozens of beef carcasses hanging on hooks ready to be butchered into a smaller room with a large bandsaw on a blood-stained chopping table. The bandsaw could slide along the length of the table. A woman and two men walked in. She had long, bright red hair and large eyes in a well lived-in face. The largest of the two men had a perfectly smooth bald head that just needed three holes drilled in it to make a perfect bowling ball, and he had a permanently angry, unpleasant look about him. The other one was the sort of typically thin, mousey, slime-bag perpetrator who spends most his life in and out of jail.

Nitro was made to take off all his clothes and they strapped him on the table, legs apart.

The woman said, 'I need to know where the microchip is. I have the one I need but I want the other one as well.'

Nitro said, 'There's a nice place waiting for people like you down in the sewer. I'll call ahead for you and tell them you're coming. I don't know anything about a microwave oven.'

'Don't be a smart-arse,' she said as she started the bandsaw. 'Now, where is the other chip, or you will be speaking in a woman's voice.'

The bandsaw was slowly being slid between Nitro's legs towards his crutch. Nitro was quietly saying goodbye to his little dolly and its two friends when the woman's phone rang.

She said, 'Get him off the table and get his jacket on.'

They hooked him up through his coat among the beef.

She said, 'With no clothes on, you will be dead before nightfall. That phone call I just received was to advise me that we have a fourth person here now to help, so we are getting some back-up security to set that up.'

Well, this is a nice mess I've got myself into! I was probably going to be better off with a woman's voice and a skirt, he said to himself. *Jesus, it's bloody cold in here.*

He thought he heard something, so he concentrated harder. Yes, there it was again.

'Who's there?' he called out. 'I can hear you. Who is it?'

A quiet female voice from behind him said, 'Be quiet. It's Lola.'

'They have all gone. Get me down. I'm freezing.'

'I was delivering a document for ASIS at the airport when

I saw you and the man with the sign. Something gave me a red flag, so I followed you here and was about to save your family jewels. From what I saw, you wouldn't get much for them. And then they suddenly left. I'm not allowed to detour when I'm on a job, but I'll drop you off somewhere. Nice to see you again, Nitro.'

He told the Spiders what had happened. They said he wouldn't be allowed out by himself in future.

*   *   *

Admiral David Seashore worked out of Russell Office in Canberra and was in charge of Australia's defence but no one had seen him for several weeks and all efforts to contact him had failed. He had been taken hostage by a section on the dark web who called themselves the Scorpions. Their three-man field operatives consisted of one woman, whose name was Scarlet, and two men, Lucifer and Mort, who Nitro had unfortunately already met. They had a fourth member who was like a roaming extra who was used from time to time.

The admiral had been anaesthetised and taken to the cabins at Hotham where he had been implanted with the chip. Immediately after the procedure, the medical staff had been eliminated and placed in the steel lockers in the basement of the second cabin by the Scorpions, as there were to be no witnesses to the implant operation. The admiral had no idea where he was now, but he knew he had been sedated. Even though he was sixty-five and his youth, fitness and strength days had long left him, it was an effort just to put one foot in front of the other. He had a wife but no children or family. He knew his wife would be worried, and he knew someone from the government would be looking for him. Why his head was sore, he had no idea.

The three Scorpions had taken up residence in an old, abandoned ten-storey sugar factory when they rang Russell Office in Canberra. They spoke to Air Marshal Robert Howser.

'We have the Admiral and by the end of the week, if we don't have $200 million, we will kill him and totally demolish Canberra. To show you what we can do, watch the five-storey abandoned building next to your office.'

They switched on the module controller. A red light came on which flashed 'Wait for green light, wait for green light.' They took the controller to the window of the door the Admiral was in so they could watch the effect of the chip. The green light came on and was flashing 'Ready, ready', so they pushed the start button and watched the Admiral go into some sort of a trance, like he had been hypnotised. They gave him the details of the building that needed to be destroyed and gave him back his phone. He punched in various code numbers and letters and then the coordinates of the old building in Canberra. Scarlet used her throw-away phone and rang the Air Marshal back.

'Are you watching?'

He could hear the missile coming and then a huge explosion. The building was now just rubble.

Scarlet said, 'The end of the week or the Admiral's dead and so is Canberra. We will be in touch' and hung up.

You think that didn't get everyone off their arse! The Chief of Joint Operations, a Vice Admiral, called an urgent meeting and who was who in the zoo was there along with all the security agencies. Some of those at the meeting found out, regardless of rank, that they actually weren't in charge of what they thought they were, and they certainly weren't the ones who had the last say. They might have been a big fish, but their pond was very small, and this high-powered meeting brought them back to some sort of reality of what size fish they actually were in the big pond.

Air Marshall Howser received a second call that said, 'If you want to help the Admiral, be at the fish markets in South Melbourne, stall 14 at midday tomorrow. It's important you're there by yourself, and don't wear your uniform.'

Howser rang Harrigan at ASIS and told him what had just happened.

He said, 'Don't worry. We will have someone there whom they will never suspect.'

His next phone call was to the Spiders, but all their phones went to message, so he would try again later.

Back at the sugar factory, the Admiral had returned to normal with no knowledge of what he had done. He had been given Kentucky Fried Chicken and a bottle of Coke. The room he was being kept in was the size of a small bedroom with a single bed, a table with one chair and a toilet and shower combination. (This room and two others had been made liveable for workers when the building was to be renovated. That decision had since been changed to demolition.)

*   *   *

Back at Fairview, Max said to Jane, 'Open the gate, please. There is a police car that wants to get in.'

All smiles, two female police officers got out and said, 'You must be important. You have been instructed to ring someone called Harrigan at the ASIS as soon as possible. We, the police here in town, didn't know we had a couple of ASIS agents living here.'

'It's a who needs to know thing, and the police don't need to know, so start forgetting you know,' Max said. 'Bloody ASIS, why don't they just use the phone like everyone else does? We have to ring them now, so what's the difference, me ringing them or them ringing me? There's no difference, is there? Sorry you had to come here just for that.'

'No problem, we have to do as we are told, just like you do, I suppose, and you're on higher ground than us.'

'Isn't that nice? Everyone is just doing what they're told!'

They drove away, smiling. They rang Harrigan and he brought them up to date. The Spiders would not be on their own this time but had been asked to help find the location of where the Scorpions were holding the Admiral. They only had till Friday, four days. There was a group committee in Canberra working on it as well as all the security agencies. He gave them a special number to ring in Canberra.

'I don't think we will be ringing a committee; you know they're responsible for the design of the poor bloody camels. I think we will tackle this one by ourselves, or have a go at it anyway. We will keep you posted of any positive results.'

The Spiders had been warned they might be required again, so when Max rang them, they were ready and would be at Fairview that night. After the usual 'Hello, what's happening, get me a drink' bantering was over, they sat down to the reason they were all at Fairview again.

'So, how do we attack this?' Wiggy said.

Slim said, 'Well, I don't know if all these nut heads have the same brain, but remember when Lola was taken hostage and taken to an old, abandoned building? I'm thinking it could be exactly the same here. So, why don't we get a list of them and start there? Hopefully they're still be here in Melbourne with the Admiral.'

They searched the internet for a list.

'I didn't realise there were so many,' said Slim.

The list included Larundel Mental Asylum, the old sugar factory, Parkdale Hospital, Box Hill Brickworks, St Kilda Vaults (small shops built into an embankment and bricked in, and not what they were looking for), Alphington Paper Mills, Bradmill cotton factory and the John Darling flour mill.

Wiggy said, 'In the morning, we each should pick one of these sites and go in pairs. Be careful if there is a car parked near the building. It could be the place we want, but don't go in by yourself. Let everyone know and we will meet you there. If it is the place, we will ring Harrigan and his mob can take it from there.'

They drew the names out of a hat. In the morning, Wiggy and Tuppence were going to the Box Hill Brickworks and Nitro and Sparkie to the Parkdale Hospital. Brewster and Auntie were going to the Larundel Mental Asylum and Slim and Slowpoke to the old sugar factory, both of which were close to each other, so they decided to all go together.

There were no vehicles anywhere near the Asylum, so they went in.

'What an awful place!' said Slowpoke. 'Imagine having to work here.'

It was quite a disturbing experience wandering through the place, but there was nothing there. They would ring the other Spiders after they had checked the sugar factory. They headed off to the old sugar factory. Around the back where the old rubbish containers and sugar drums was a Toyota commercial van with the hire company logo on the side, 'Vans R Us' concealed between the containers.

'Well,' said Slim, 'this is certainly looking positive. I would love to go in and look around.'

'Well, you will certainly be going in' – they spun around – 'but there will be no looking around,' said Scarlet, who had got the jump on them.

Lucifer came out from behind the containers. Mort was upstairs, watching the Admiral.

Jesus, Slim said to himself, *these are the ones who have the Admiral.*

'So, what are you doing here and who are you?' the woman said. She had a thin face, green, searching eyes and the reddest hair you would ever see.

Slim said, 'We belong to a club called Urbex.'

'What does that mean?' said the other bloke, who reminded Slowpoke of a ferret with his long, thin face, small, round, brown eyes, long nose and small jagged teeth.

Slowpoke said, 'It refers to people who like looking at and in old abandon buildings. And that's what we were doing. It's of no concern to us whatever it is you're doing.'

'Well, that may be so,' the woman said, 'but just in case, you're coming with us.'

They were escorted up to the second floor, searched, their phones taken and asked why they had guns.

They said, 'For protection from people like you.'

'That didn't go too well, did it?' Scarlet said.

'To quote someone I know,' Slim said, 'it's not over till the fat lady sings. And when that happens, young lady, you will be history.'

They were kept in a room identical to the one the Admiral was in; they saw him when they came in. The mistake Scarlet made was that she did not take their watches, and Brewster's watch was also a phone. They tried ringing Harrigan, but his voicemail said he wasn't taking calls. They rang the special number they'd been given; it was answered by a grade 3 clerk who said, 'We are not taking any calls today; the committee is in lockdown.'

Christ,' Brewster said, 'the government officials are as useless as tits on a bull.'

'So, the sheriff and his posse aren't coming?' Slim said.

'I'm running short on watch power, so I'm ringing our own Batman and Robin and the Wonder Girls.'

Brewster rang Wiggy who said, 'Save the watch battery. We'll come. I can't tell you when, but we will be there. Why do I have to keep rescuing that idiot, Slim? Tell him his dad's coming to save him from the bullies.'

'I heard that smart-arse remark,' Slim yelled out.

Wiggy said to Nitro and Tuppence, 'Brewster said they were on the second floor of a ten-storey building. There are only three of them, one woman and two men, but they have the ground floor and outside surrounding area covered, so we have to come up with a plan to get in and not get our mob and the Admiral killed. Start thinking, you three. As usual, we're getting no help from Harrigan's mob. They're not taking any calls – can you believe that! We could all be eliminated by little people from space, and they wouldn't have a clue what was happening. Bloody oxygen thieves, the lot of them.'

'Nitro has found the address on the internet and the building has a large flat roof. Dare we mention this for our own safety?' said Auntie, 'We all shit ourselves last time we flew with you, Wiggy, but it seems the only way – to come over the top and land on the roof.'

'Do *we* have to go in the helicopter?' the girls said.

Wiggy and Nitro both said, 'Yes, you do.'

'Oh, shit!' they said. 'We're scared just thinking about it.'

Wiggy rang and booked a Robby R 44 for the next day.

* * *

When Scarlet and her goons were gone, Slim and the Admiral could talk to each other through the thin wall. The Admiral had no idea why he had been taken or where he was, so Slim told him all about the FLC chip and why his head was sore, and that they had already used him as a demonstration to blow up an abandoned building.

Slim said, 'You don't remember anything afterwards, it's like being hypnotised, and once you're under, there's nothing you can do about it. There's only one way and that's to somehow get the control module off them, and at the moment that's not looking good. The only other way is that our Spider heroes arrive to save the day, and that's not looking too good either.'

The Spiders arrived at Essendon Airport and Wiggy produced his licence. He was told he was at the top of his rating, but he wasn't licensed for anything larger. Yeah, well, he had news for them, didn't he? They went down to a black Robby 44 and Wiggy went through the external and internal preflight checks and start-up procedures.

'Okay,' Wiggy said, 'we're all good to go. All aboard.'

Nitro climbed in, but the girls just stood there.

'Come on, get in.'

'Oh, we're not going. We just came to wave goodbye.'

'You are going. Now, get in before this thing shakes me to death.'

Wiggy lifted off with three white-knuckled passengers. They flew out over St Kilda beach.

Maria said, 'This is a nice little helicopter, Wiggy, and you're good at flying this one. I haven't wet my pants this time, but I'd like to go back now.'

Nitro said, 'Shut up, Sparkie. We are not going back, so just enjoy the flight.'

'There it is, down there,' Wiggy said, 'We need to fly in, hover on top and land quickly, as these things make a lot of noise from the outside.'

They landed and shut down all systems.

Wiggy said to Sparkie, 'You're staying here to mind the chopper. Anyone who comes up on this roof who's not a Spider, shoot to kill. Don't muck around.'

Wiggy rang Brewster's watchphone but only for two rings. He knew Brewster's watch only buzzed, so unless someone else was in the room, it should be all right. He sent Brewster a text message: *We are in like Flynn. On the top floor, there are stairs at either end of the building. I'm going down one end and Nitro and Tuppence the other end. It might take a while to get to you but we're on our way.*

'We still need to talk to each other but turn your phones to buzz mode. Let's go get our Spiders back. Stay connected with each other and share your progress,' said Wiggy.

All the action would be on the second floor, and they couldn't see anyone climbing stairs for no reason. They would have no problems going down. When they arrived on the second floor, they texted each other with their locations.

There were lots of rooms for concealment as they worked their way along the corridor. Some were for storage, others had machines in them and one was an administration block. Towards the end of the corridor, they were close enough to each other they could now give hand signals. They could hear Mort talking on the phone.

'I'm going to get the food for lunch. I'll lock the door when I go. No need for Lucifer to come up from watching the front of the building.'

Mort had come out of the door and locked it when Tuppence shot him clean through his ear into his brain. Nitro dragged him down the corridor and hid him in one of the machine rooms. He searched him for the door key, but no luck.

Wiggy spoke to them through the door and said, 'It will make too much noise if we break down the door. Just hang on in there while we even the score and bring the numbers down out here.'

* * *

Harrigan asked everyone in the emergency room if they'd had any contact on the Spiders' special phone. Everyone shook their heads, but the young clerk said, 'Someone did ring on that phone, and I told them we were not taking any calls today until further notice.'

'Jesus, who told you that?'

Someone said, 'I told him that, but I said with the exception of the red phone.'

Harrigan said, 'Look, I know these people might be old but they're bloody good. They should be in here and half of you out there digging bloody holes somewhere. If I know them, they've found the Admiral and are having lunch and a wine with him at Portsea or somewhere.'

He rang the numbers he had for the Spiders. They all went to message except Sparkie's because she had her phone on ring as she was on the roof. She told him what she knew.

He said, 'Where are you?'

She said she didn't know because Wiggy had flown them here, and from the sky she had no idea where she was. She was minding the helicopter on the roof.

'Jesus,' Harrigan said, 'is there anything you old bastards can't do?'

Maria said, 'Doesn't look like it, does it?'

Harrigan said, 'When you get a chance, get Wiggy or Slim to ring me urgently.'

* * *

Scarlet said to Lucifer, 'Have you seen Mort? He shouldn't have been this long. Go up and see if he is back yet.'

Wiggy heard him coming up the stair. He waited, hidden in an alcove on the second-floor landing.

Wiggy came out of hiding, pointing his gun at Lucifer and said, 'Hello, what's your name?'

'Lucifer.'

'Can you fly like me, Lucifer? Because it's time you learnt.'

Wiggy pushed him over the landing rail. He hit the ground head first and broke his neck.

Scarlet realised it was all turning to shit. She rang her roaming agent and told him to come and get the control module from where she had hidden it.

The room opposite where the Spiders were being held had

their guns and phones, so that was handy.

Nitro called out, 'Get away from the door. We're coming in.'

They shot the lock off and broke in. The Admiral's room was next, and out he came. They could hear the red-headed woman coming up the stairs, screaming, 'Get going, everyone, up to the roof. You too, Admiral.' They all hit the stairs at the other end of the building while Scarlet was running up the front stairs.

Wiggy said, 'Slim, when we get to the roof, you keep her inside firing at the door till I get back. Ten minutes, that's all. Any three of you, get in.'

Wiggy flipped the switches, the rotors spun and he took them all down to the cars in three trips. On the last trip, Scarlet had got out on the roof through another door and was standing on top of an air conditioner, firing at the chopper. Wiggy said to himself, *I've had enough of you, blood nut.* He swung the chopper round and the tail with the rear rotor cut down through the top of her head and halfway down her back. Current score: Spiders three, enemy nil.

Auntie and Sparkie didn't want to return in the chopper, but Tuppence and Slowpoke did, so Wiggy said he would take the two girls and the Admiral. The others would take the cars and go somewhere for lunch. Wiggy would arrange with the Admiral where they would be staying that night.

Wiggy said, 'I'll call you when to pick us up at Essendon Airport.'

Sparkie said, 'I forgot to tell you. Harrigan wants you or Slim to ring him urgently.'

'Jesus, how long ago was that?'

'About two hours ago.'

'I'll be seeing him at Portsea. The police helicopter and their pad is at the Portsea police station, so if the Admiral doesn't mind, he can ring them and get a clearance to land, and they can join us for lunch at the Portsea pub which is almost next door. I'll ring Harrigan and he can drive down and meet us while he's in Melbourne.'

When Harrigan arrived, the Admiral said, 'Have we got anyone in the system as good as these retirees?'

'Probably not,' said Harrigan.

'Well, we better look after them. Where are you all staying tonight?'

'We've not booked in anywhere yet,' said Wiggy, 'Been a bit busy.'

'Right,' said the Admiral, 'When us shiny arses come to Melbourne, we stay at the Crown Towers. Harrigan will book you all in at government expense with a spending limit of $5000 for the group. I will be speaking to the prime minister about the Spiders. How old did you say you all were?'

'Seventies and eighties,' said Wiggy.

'Jesus, I can't believe your fitness and expertise! Max, I wouldn't call you a gun pilot mate but you're doing okay.'

Jane pressed the talk button on only the pilot's helmet and said, 'Fly me to the moon, honey, and we can dream and play with the stars.'

Chapter 12

They were invited to the lodge to meet the prime minister. ASIS, and MI6 representatives, the Minister for Defence and other hanger-ons were also there. They would have normally been given awards but because of the nature of the top-secret mission, they were getting bugger all. The Spiders would talk to the prime minister when they got him on his own. As far as a financial reward was concerned, this wasn't over till the fat lady had sung.

The Admiral was in hospital having the chip removed. They hadn't known him long, but it seemed the right thing to do to visit him in hospital, to say thank you for the lovely accommodation and the expense money. The Son of God Hospital was a five-storey building, built in 1956, that was looking its age now, but the hospital had a very good name for specialised treatment. The information desk told them he was in room 416 on the fourth floor, so they caught the lift and went up.

The nurse there told them he had just gone to theatre, but she was happy for them to watch through the glass viewing window outside the theatre. There were two doctors and two theatre nurses, and another woman was standing to one side. Wiggy wondered why she was there as she didn't seem to have a job.

The anaesthetist put the Admiral to sleep, and the chip was removed just as an Iroquois helicopter appeared at the window. The woman in the theatre shot everyone except the Admiral. She opened the window so that a cable with a canvas bag attached to it could come in though the window. The chip was placed in the bag and was pulled back into the chopper. The safety harness was brought in and fastened to the Admiral. The helicopter hovering outside the window was now winding the cable in and dragged the Admiral, still under the anaesthetic, off the table on to the floor and was pulling him towards the aircraft.

The Spiders couldn't believe what they were seeing. Slim and Wiggy rushed in. Wiggy gave the woman the old Liverpool kiss with his head, broke her nose and knocked her out. They pushed her out the window and she went five floors to her death.

The Admiral was still being dragged towards the window. Slim grabbed him but too late to unfasten the harness. Out the window went the Admiral, with Slim hanging on to him. There was only one other person apart from the pilot and he was operating the winch. As they got close to the chopper, Slim grabbed the skid rail as the winch operator hauled the Admiral into the aircraft. Slim was now hanging on like some kid on the monkey bars, with his legs wrapped around the skids. The winch operator leaned out to see if Slim was still there. Slim grabbed him, pulled him out and watched him spiralling down like a kite. He had a hell of a job getting into the chopper, but at last he made it.

They were now flying out over St Kilda beach when the radio squawked in the pilot's helmet. He said, 'Roger that', and threw out of the chopper a small bag attached to a parachute with the chip and monitor inside. Slim found a spear gun mounted on the fuselage. He fired it into the back of the pilot's seat, and it came out his stomach.

There were now no feet on the torque pedals or hands on the cyclic and collective, so the chopper began to spin like a top. Slim managed to jump out before the chopper hit the water and began to sink. He dived down to rescue the Admiral, but he was too heavy to bring to the surface. Slim was out of breath, and he had to get to the surface and leave the Admiral behind to drown with the pilot. He was disappointed that he had not been as strong as he used to be, and now he would have the Admiral's death on his mind as a failure on his behalf. A fishing boat picked him up and Slim borrowed the man's phone to ring Wiggy who rang Harrigan. Divers retrieved the body of the Admiral and the pilot.

*　*　*

It was a perfect day for a funeral if you were making a movie, overcast with local showers. The ladies all wore black outfits, and there were black umbrellas everywhere. The service and words that were spoken were typical, specially prepared military bullshit, followed by a seventeen-gun salute with the pomp and glory required of an Admiral. The Spiders had not known him long but the time they had known him was special. They saw Harrigan talking to a middle-aged woman who came over and introduced herself as the Admiral's wife. She thanked them for all the support and risks they had taken for her husband.

Slowpoke said, 'You're very welcome, and we are so sorry for your loss.'

Harrigan had taken the opportunity at the funeral to fill Wiggy in on the latest problem. All this was about the security of the bloody FLC taken from the Admiral's head and the control module taken from the old sugar factory.

I think we should use one of the Spiders. They will be seen as just one of the shoppers at the fish market.'

'I agree,' said Wiggy, 'but there is safety in numbers. You know how we operate – one in, all in. We will spread ourselves around the market somewhere near the fish stall, and if anything goes wrong, we'll have the numbers when is all this happening. Tomorrow at midday, we'll be there. Tell the air marshal we will all have something red on, like a flower, scarf, tie or hat, so he will know where his support is.'

The next day at 11.30 am they were all in place around the fish market. As it got closer to midday, they had all walked past stall 14 once and looked at the fish for sale. That gave the Air Marshal a chance to see who they all were.

At midday, a man appeared and approached another man who must have been the Air Marshal. He was wearing the same sort of overalls the fish sellers wore. He was around six feet tall and his bald head was being kept warm by a thin layer of fur and a black beret. He had a cruel face and large calcified hands. It looked like he was about to shake hands with Howser, but he snapped on a handcuff attached to his own wrist and his left hand was on a gun under his jacket. His name was Cripto.

The problem now was if they rushed him, he could kill Howser. This was now beginning to piss off the Spiders.

Cripto had informed the authorities if they came after the chips, he would dispose of Howser.

They spoke to Harrigan who said, 'You know the game – follow discreetly, don't get him killed.'

They followed him into Southern Cross train station, where he went to the ticketing window and then left with Howser still attached. Nitro followed them while the Spiders produced their ID and found out what tickets he had bought –two gold class double tickets to Darwin on The Ghan, leaving the next night. The Spiders rang Harrigan and he purchased four double Platinum Class cabins. They had managed to convince him that being in a different class would keep them away and less chance of detection. He knew that was bullshit but they were friends, good people and good at what they did, and they deserved the extra comfort with all the risks they took.

They went home to pack. Slim said, 'Don't forget your guns.'

The Overland train to Adelaide wouldn't get them there in time to catch The Ghan that left at 12.15 pm. So, Cripto was obviously flying, and so now were the Spiders, in an ASIS private business class Boeing jet operated by No. 34 Squadron RAAF.

Slim said, 'Make the most of it, because it will be the first and last time you will ever fly in that.'

The girls were excited but hesitant. They were thinking about their last train trip. This one wouldn't be as up market as the Orient Express, but it was supposed to be very nice, and they were really looking forward to it. Harrigan had organised two Commonwealth cars to take them and their luggage from their motels to the airport. The Ghan staff escorted them to their cabins and told them what time breakfast was; the Platinum Club Lounge would be open till 11 pm and they could get a snack and a drink in there if they wished. The boys went for a drink, and the girls stayed in their cabins, which were large and comfortable. They were looking for a good night's sleep. They knew in the morning all bets would be off.

The problem would be how to get Howser away from Cripto.

Meanwhile, Air Marshal Howser said to Cripto, 'Are you crazy? You will have the whole Australian army after you.'

'Shut up or you'll get no breakfast', and he handcuffed him to the toilet pipes. As he left, he said, 'And you haven't met my friend yet either.'

The Spiders were in the dining car for breakfast in their pairs, sitting separately at tables with other travellers, so to anyone, it all looked quite normal. Cripto came in and sat at a table with another man who was sitting by himself, an average looking man but with that telltale bulge in his jacket, and the same expression on his face as an egg. As much as they tried not to show it, they certainly knew each other, so now it looked like the Spiders had two to contend with.

It just gets harder all the time, Slim said to himself.

The Spiders were in cabins 14 to 17 and Cripto and Howser were in cabin 4 in the next carriage. As he had a Gold Class ticket, he shouldn't have been in their dining car.

Wiggy said, 'I'll speak to the dining car and club car attendants, and they can tell him he has to play somewhere else. And let's find out if Egg Head is only gold class as well.'

Although they had given him no reason to be suspicious, they didn't want to have him watching their every move.

Anything they had to do would be done when the train stopped, and the handcuffs were removed.

There were eight of them who could wander past his cabin or go into his club car every now and then to get an idea what he was doing with Howser and where he might be keeping him. They might have transferred him into Egg Head's cabin.

'We need to find out where that is,' said Auntie.

They had been on the train now for two days. Slim thought, *Last night's dinner was a fabulous four-course meal accompanied by wines and champagne, and the breakfasts are magnificent. How can they prepare meals like this on a bloody train?*

Between Manguri and Alice Springs, Egg Head and Cripto had been swapping cabins in Gold Class back and forth for two days. At Alice Springs, Cripto got off the train to look around and then got back on. Egg Head now got off and wandered the full length of the train, thirty-six carriages and about 700 metres long. Slim walked with him from inside the train, through all the carriages. When he got to the end, he got out and found Egg Head pretending to have a wee. What he was really doing was tying a small black bag on to the back of the train, onto a small U-bolt low to the ground. He had his back to Slim, so Slim smacked him over the head and down he went. Slim searched him to find out who he was and put his wallet and phone in his pocket. He took the small bag, and he also found a set of handcuffs in Egg Head's pocket. With a cheesy grin, Slim padlocked his arms to the U-bolt. The big diesel engine blew its horns, indicating a five-minute warning to get back on the train. Egg Head could scream all he wanted; no one would hear him way back there. When the train next stopped, Egg Head would be dead, and he would also have no legs.

They were rolling again towards Darwin. Cripto was wandering up and down the passageways looking for Egg Head who had the handcuffs in his pocket. He went back to his cabin and told the Air Marshal that when they got to Darwin, he would be using a dressing-gown belt to tie them together, and if he considered there was a threat, he would definitely shoot him.

The Spiders were amazed. Inside the small bag was the control module. It had obviously been tied to the train for someone to pick up at the next stop.

Slowpoke said, 'See, they're doing it again, separating the parts of the package. Well, they won't know we have the control module, will they?'

Egg Head's wallet said his name was Trent Duvall from Belarus, so it smelled like the Russians had engaged Scarlet and the Scorpions to retrieve the chip, implant it into someone for a trial to make sure it was the correct chip, then remove it and deliver the complete FLC package back to Russia. But they didn't have the full package.

The Ghan arrived in Katherine, where they assumed the black bag was supposed to be collected. The Spiders watched Cripto walk down towards the back of the train. When he arrived, he almost vomited. Trent Duvall's body was gone from the stomach down, with sinews, bones and skin hanging down from where the ground couldn't reach the body anymore. Cripto now knew his days alive were limited once the Russians found out he had lost part of the package. Or maybe the little black bag had already been picked up by the right person. Although that was unlikely, he could always hope.

The Spiders were in Slim and Slowpoke's cabin working on the next move and checking all the phone numbers and received messages in Trent's phone's memory. There was one particularly interesting message that said. *On the train, stay incognito. Dining car looks good, Trent. Sounds good, 021236780, Cripto, 7 pm.* They rang Harrigan and gave him the plan.

'Sounds risky,' he said, 'but go ahead and give it a go, but don't lose or hinder the rest of the group's cover.'

They rang Cripto's number.

Slim said in a rough voice, 'Have you got it all?'

Cripto's voice trembled as he said, 'I think I have lost the module, and Trent is dead.'

'What! You brainless bastard! If you don't find it, you're dead also. We will take control of the chip before you lose that. When the train gets into Darwin, you will hand over Howser and the chip to one of our agents. His name is Slim Drargo. He will have a red scarf and a red skin mark down his left cheek. He will say, "Where can you get hot chips here?" and you will answer, "Here at the station". Then save your life by getting off your arse and finding the module. You have forty-eight hours. Don't stuff this up!"

The Spiders rang Harrigan who said, 'A gunship will lift off in half an hour and will be there before you.'

Slim said, 'Make sure there is someone whom the Air Marshal knows for positive recognition, and tell them to get him on that whirly bird quick time. I will pass on the chip to whoever is in charge. Please advise me who that will be.'

When they got off the train, Slim had a red highlighter pen mark on his face, and went round in a wide circle to make it look like he was coming from outside and not off the train. He spotted Cripto almost immediately. Slim thought that Howser knew who he was as well. The exchange went without a hitch. There were only two people at the handover, including the

Commander's secretary whose name was Day Dadaty. Dadaty was a funny little man; it was almost as if he wasn't there at all.

'Hello, Day,' said Howser.

'Hello, sir,' said Day.

Later, the chips and module were handed over to a woman named Shelly Artween.

Slim said, 'Now, get out of here as fast as you can.'

Harrigan wanted to fly them home but the Spiders wanted to go back by train so they could relax this time and enjoy the trip without any stress.

Cripto sat at the station in Darwin thinking about his last forty-eight hours to live, because he had no idea where the module had gone, and now the whole package had gone. *If the Russians know that, I won't even have forty-eight hours*, he thought. You could see Cripto was really pissed off. Suddenly he realised where he had seen this man before. It was the red scarf that triggered it. He had seen him at the fish market, and there was a chance he had also been on the train. But whose side was he on? He could have been a contract agent for the Russians, or he could be an enemy agent.

Harrigan had used his authority to get four more cabins on The Ghan back to Adelaide. Unfortunately, that meant some people who thought they were going on the train weren't. Cripto had seen Slim and a lot of other people getting their tickets.

Shit, he said to himself, *he's going back on the train with the package.*

Cripto could only get a single Gold Class ticket as the whole train was booked out. He swore but bought the ticket. He would track down this skinny smart-arse and get the package back. He would get on the train early and go into his cabin until the train was moving. That way Slim wouldn't know he was on the train until it was too late. Unfortunately for Cripto, the package wasn't on the train, and he didn't know that Slim wasn't on his own.

The Spiders piled back on the train, ready for a fantastic trip back, with lovely food and wine and relaxation in the club car, with the scenery of the desert through the large windows. It doesn't get any better than this, they said. That night they decided to dress up a bit for dinner and then go to the club car for after-dinner drinks and some port with a game of cards. Tuppence wore a casual but chic, soft open-fronted long-sleeved cardigan over a V-necked maxi cami dress in a leaf pattern with matching sandals. Slowpoke wore a two-piece ensemble, a sophisticated open-fronted jacket over a vibrant floral tank dress with comfortable, pastel green mid-heel shoes. Auntie chose a comfortable, versatile and stylish three-piece outfit with long sleeves, open-fronted cardigan, a V-necked sleeveless tank top and wide leg pants. Sparkie wore a three-quarter sleeved, crew necked pants suit in a nice pastel buttercup colour in a Middle Eastern style. Nitro, Slim and Wiggy all wore dark blue sports jackets with silver and gold buttons and light grey sports pants. Brewster had on his usual white business long-sleeved shirt tucked into the elastic waistband of his long linen pants; he was never going to be a male model. (Brewster and Wiggy have their own different ideas on fashion.)

The dining car looked fantastic. The lights were dim and the soft music playing was the song 'When a child is born'. They were shown to two tables of four. The lights from the train windows lit up part of the desert as it rushed by. It was all very pleasant.

Halfway through the meal, someone said, 'Can anyone smell smoke?'

They were right, and the smoke was getting thicker.

Slim and Nitro said, 'It's coming from the kitchen.'

They went to investigate with the steward and found the kitchen hand dead on the floor. There was writing carved on both his arms that read, 'If you don't hand over the package, you're next.' The smoke was coming through a wide open door from a wood fire with a pan on the hot plate that was on fire.

'Who is on the train that would do that to a kitchen hand?' said Tuppence.

'I'll have the police on board as soon as we reach Alice Springs,' said the steward.

After dinner, the Spiders went to the club car as planned.

Auntie said, 'I can't believe I'm going to tell you this, but I think I saw that awful man called Cripto on the train.'

'No,' said Slim, 'I left him on the station at Darwin.'

'But did you actually see him on the platform as we left?' asked Brewster.

'Well, no.'

'Then he could be on the train, couldn't he, particularly if he thinks you have got the package. After the handover, he wasn't actually there to see who got to keep the package, was he? I would say he thinks you have the package, and he wants it back before the Russians kill him for being an oxygen thief and a dickhead. Well, this is a fine kettle of fish, isn't it?'

* * *

Cripto made some phone calls to someone he knew. He was

smart enough to know that Slim was part of a group of people who were probably all agents. But it was dangerous territory.

Auntie was in the habit of exercising by walking the long length of the train. When she walked past Cripto's cabin, he grabbed her and dragged her inside.

'Where is the package?' he said.

'We don't have it. It's with the government.'

'Bullshit!' he said and injected her with a sleeper that would last till they arrived in Alice Springs. Even if she woke up there, she would be dopey.

*   *   *

Auntie had been off the grid now for a couple of hours. Brewster was very worried, knowing that bastard Cripto was on board.

'There is no other reason she would be missing,' he said.

Auntie was out like a light, so Cripto could leave his cabin. He gave a note to the steward in the dining cabin to give to the group when they came in. It said, 'I have the woman and if I don't have the package by the time we reach Alice Springs, I will dump her where she will never be found. She will die a long and painful death.'

The Spiders read the note, and Wiggy put it in his pocket.

Brewster said, 'I'm going to kill him after I've squashed his nuts with a hammer.'

'Well, that won't be happening till we get Auntie back,' they said, 'so, any ideas?'

'He obviously thinks we have the package, and telling him we haven't won't help. It will probably just make it worse.'

There were lots of things you could do when The Ghan

got to Alice Springs. You could take a helicopter ride over the MacDonnell Ranges and Simpsons Gap in the Red Centre, but the Spiders had more pressing things on their minds. When they arrived in Alice Springs, Cripto was dragging a half-conscious Auntie towards a black helicopter. The Spiders ran to The Ghan's helicopter tour office which had a chopper wound up and standing by for tourists from The Ghan. They showed them their ASIS identification and ran to the chopper. They could only take four, so the boys went, much to the pleasure of the girls. The pilot had been given the bare bones of what was happening.

Cripto and Auntie were up there somewhere, but you can't hide from radar, and that's what was happening now. They could see the other chopper now and it looked like it had just taken off, but it had actually hovered about three feet off the ground. Cripto had thrown Auntie out and was climbing again. The problem was there was no room for Auntie in the Spiders' chopper.

Wiggy said, 'Land and pick her up, and I'll wait for you to come back for me.'

Brewster said, 'No, mate. I'll go and wait.'

'No, you stay here and tend to your wife.'

As they hovered a foot off the deck, Wiggy said to Auntie, 'Get in quick. I'm staying.'

As she got in, she said, 'Watch out for the giant ants.' She already had two bites on her legs.

The pilot said, 'We will be back in an hour.'

Up they went and banked away.'

Jesus, that hurt! What was that? Wiggy thought as a big lump appeared on his leg. He looked down to see half a dozen giant red bull ants as big as his little finger on his shoe. They were all around for ten or twenty metres. The ground was covered with them. He saw some dry wood and branches not far away, so he made a dash for them, trying to jump from one small clear patch to another. He looked like an idiot learning to ballet dance.

The fact that he still had a cigarette lighter in his pocket was just simply God's gift. So was the note in his pocket. Ants were all over the wood, but they didn't last long once the fire got going. So now he had a small circle next to the fire with no ants. He could hear the chopper coming back, which was very reassuring, considering he was somewhere in the Red Centre with a million giant ants.

Next thing, there was a hail of bullets. It was the chopper with Cripto. Wiggy was forced to leave his safe place by the fire and the ants to find cover somewhere. All that was left was climbing a tree and burning the ants one by one with the cigarette lighter as they climbed the tree after him. He now had about ten bites on his legs and the pain was unbearable. He heard a rustle and looked up to see a very large and angry bird with a wingspan of eight feet had landed in the tree above him. The jabiru had seen Wiggy near its exceptionally large and deep nest. Above his head, Wiggy saw a little bald head and a little long beak looking over the top of the nest. The jabiru was working its way down the tree to protect the baby bird. Wiggy said to himself, *Mate, I think you're fucked.*

The chopper had stopped firing – Cripto obviously couldn't get a good look at him in the tree – and then he heard the other chopper coming back. They landed with the boys still on board. Thankfully, the chopper had frightened the jabiru away. It took off like a small light aircraft but kept circling the tree. Cripto's chopper had also banked away.

Wiggy said, 'ASIS is now commandeering this helicopter.'

The pilot said, What?'

'Take it up with the government, and get in the back. What's your name?'

'Rex.'

When Wiggy got in the pilot's seat, the boys said, 'Shit, not again! You're going to get the ride of your life, mate. This bloke can't fly; he makes it up as he goes along.'

Wiggy took a minute to look around. It wasn't much different to what he was used to, and besides, he had the dude in the back seat who could give him some advice if he needed it. Wiggy gently pulled on the collective and they lifted off, using the cyclic to eliminate any drift in direction and the pedals to maintain the chopper's balance. The real pilot showed Wiggy how to operate the radar equipment, and there it was, the black helicopter some distance away, waiting for them.

Wiggy said, 'What are those things on the radar?'

Rex said, 'They are wind turbine generators.'

'Christ, look how many there are!'

'Yes,' said Rex, 'there are 300 of them out there over ten kilometres.'

Wiggy flew the chopper in among the blades that were as big as jumbo jets wings, and lowered the chopper down low into a hover position between the blades of two of them. And they waited.

Slim said, 'Here they are now.'

Wiggy waited till they were nearly overhead and popped up in front of them. The pilot panicked and banked away into one of the wind turbine blades. It split the helicopter in two, and down it went, hitting the ground in flames.

'Shit, Wiggy, we take it all back, mate. We will fly with you anytime.'

When they got back to Alice Springs, there was thirty minutes left before The Ghan left.

Wiggy said, 'Can I take the chopper for a last flight with my wife?'

'Mate, the way you fly on sheer instinct, take it. And don't come back to Alice Springs or I'll be out of a job.'

Wiggy and Tuppence lifted off and flew over Simpsons Gap.

On their way back, Tuppence said, 'You know I will love you forever, so fly me to the moon and we will be in peace among the stars forever, Max.'

They took the chopper back and promised that they would ensure that the government would pay whatever the cost was.

Things were at last looking good – no more microchips, no more ampoules, just the last day and a half of peace and serenity. They were back on the train again and looking forward to some nice meals and the view out the windows.

There was Lola.

'Jesus,' Slim said, 'what are you doing here?'

'I'm like the ASIS post lady. I got on at Alice Springs.'

Tuppence said, 'As long as there are no more bogeymen on the train, you're welcome to join us for the evening meal.'

She said she would love to.

They were starting to feel their age now, all of them. There wasn't one of them who didn't have a pain somewhere. All their parents had passed away and most of their schoolfriends, so they really only had each other now. It was really ridiculous to do what they had been doing at their age, particularly if one of them was killed or seriously injured. But each one in all their lives had been exceptionally good at whatever they had turned their hand to, and together they formed an impregnable barrier that had proven itself over and over. Sometimes they would forget just how good they were.

Max said, 'We're all getting older day by day, just like that beach down there, with the grains of sand getting blown away, grain by grain, until the ones that were there are now gone.'

So, did they want to die in a rocking chair on the veranda or shot in the head by a bullet?

The girls said, 'Well, we're getting too old to be balancing sex in a rocking chair, so it might be a win for the bullet.'

When they arrived back in Melbourne on the Overland, there was Harrigan with two government staff cars waiting for them.

Harrigan said, 'You old buggers, you're hard to keep up with, but you've come out winning again. It's time to go home and smell the roses. It's a shame you're not still eighteen. I could kiss you all.'

'Well, why don't you?' said Slowpoke.

'If he comes near me, I'll thump him,' said Nitro.

Harrigan gave the girls a welcome home kiss and said, 'There are cars waiting to take you locals home, and a chopper at Williamstown to take Max and Jane to Lakes Entrance.'

When Max and Jane flew into the small airport at Lakes Entrance, a Jabiru J230D aircraft flew past and on its fuselage were the words, 'Welcome Home, Spiders.'

Epilogue

The Spiders hired a mobility scooter for Slim who had damaged both his knees when he had hit the water, and they made sure ASIS got the bill. They were still somewhat mesmerised that, apart from Sparkie, they had all come through virtually unscathed. At their age, someone was sure to have had a stroke or heart attack, or been shot. They had told Harrigan, provided they were all still alive, they would be happy to help any time they were asked. Lieutenant Commander Harrigan was now a personal friend of the Spiders and came to all the get-togethers every three months.

The Spiders went back to using their real names, and after their last escapades, settled back into a boring lifestyle.

Max said, 'We are only a bunch of old buggers, but I am proud to call them all my friends. And who knows what the future may hold for the Spiders in time to come?'

About the Author

When **Max Thornton** writes his books, there will always be somewhere between the lines a resemblance to real life difficulties, sometimes a win and sometimes a loss. He writes with passion and has the ability to feel the words as they hit the page. He writes with no plan; the story will come from his mind or his heart, and often gives the reader that uncanny and scary way of a *déja vu* experience. He and Jane are in retirement at their property at Fairview, which they call their holy ground. They fish, travel and vote.

HARDLY
A CHALLENGE
A story of
love, sadness,
determination
and encouragement
MAX THORNTON